Curious

The Finn Factor, Book 1

R.G. ALEXANDER

Curious

Copyright © 2015 R.G. Alexander
Editing by D.S. Editing
Formatted by IRONHORSE Formatting

ISBN: 1508655960
ISBN-13: 978-1508655961

DEDICATION

Cookie-Love is the Reason

AND

Ode to Robin L Rotham

You kick my ass and make me cry

You answer each time I ask "Whyyy?"

The red marks that you leave behind

Flay my pride but fill my mind

With ways to make you LOL

Oh dearest friend, you edit well.

CHAPTER ONE

The lights at the edge of the dock flickered on as the last of the day disappeared. Jeremy stared at the still lake as it absorbed the vibrant shades of orange, gold and pink from the sunset until all those colors faded, leaving behind only blacks and blues. The darker colors suited his mood.

He was so lost in his brooding and watching the transition of color through his kitchen window that he nearly dropped his beer in the sink when he heard the knock at his front door. "Damn it."

Owen was here.

He lifted the bottle to his lips and drank until there was nothing left, then set it on the counter more forcefully than necessary while he debated whether or not to reach for his third of the hour.

It wasn't helping. The view, the color study, the buzz from the tequila and beer he'd downed on an empty stomach—nothing was relaxing him the way it usually did. He was tense about tonight. Jumpier than he should be.

Owen's thirty-fifth birthday. Any other year and he'd be at the Finn family pub by now, drinking and playing darts with the Owen's brothers, teasing their baby sister about her upcoming wedding, and watching Owen revel in his favorite tradition—kissing every woman in the establishment he wasn't related to. Because he was Irish, he'd tell them with a smile. "Every damn day."

But not this year.

The second knock sounded impatient, and Jeremy ran his hands over his face, smoothing his full beard before he walked toward the door. This year Owen had called and asked if he could hang out at Jeremy's instead. No party. No shamrock-shaped cake covered in lewd candles. No women for him to kiss and charm and take home for an all-night celebration.

It wasn't that big a deal, he told himself. Between construction jobs and girlfriends, Owen came over so much he might as well live here. It had been like that since Jeremy bought the four-bedroom home on the lake. It had more space than his own Spartan bachelor pad, and he could walk outside and go fishing or swimming whenever the mood struck him. Owen loved the place almost as much as he did, and Jeremy had to admit he enjoyed the company.

What was messing with his head were the weeks of silence that preceded this last-minute visit. Weeks when Owen hadn't done much more than answer texts with short, noncommittal replies. He hadn't stopped by after work or called to harass him into leaving the house and coming out for a drink or going to see a movie the way he usually did. Hadn't taken temporary ownership of Jeremy's big-screen television to watch a football game. Close to three weeks when Jeremy hadn't had the nerve to end the blackout himself, accepting the excuse of Owen's busy work schedule, though he knew the real reason for his absence.

Bracing himself, Jeremy opened the door, seeing the familiar logo on a large pizza box as Owen pushed it toward his chest and brushed past him. "What took you so long? Daydreaming again? I brought dinner."

His lips twitched and he shook his head. "I was going to order from the Indian restaurant."

He followed Owen down the hall and into the kitchen where his friend opened the refrigerator and pulled out two bottles of beer. "I figured. We'll eat that spicy mystery stew you love so much for *your* birthday. Tonight, it's my slumber party and I say we dine on mushrooms, pepperoni and cheese." He sent him a hopeful grin. "And Xbox?"

"Sure." Jeremy snorted, his tense shoulders relaxing a little. Owen didn't seem upset. It was almost as if nothing had happened. Nothing had changed. "I thought you turned thirty-five today, not sixteen."

"Says the man who draws comics for a living."

"That comeback never gets old. Grab the paper plates from the pantry and some napkins, please."

"Yes, Mother," followed the dramatic sigh.

Jeremy snuck a glance as Owen opened the pantry and dug around for the plates, displaying his oh so tight end. Still sexy after all these years.

Owen Finn had been the hot high school quarterback with good grades, crystal-blue eyes and a thousand-watt smile. The guy every girl on campus had wanted to date, and time had only increased his appeal.

The owner of Finn Construction had laugh lines that had deepened over the years and his work had given him a warm, healthy tan and bleached his dark blond hair with strands of gold. He was a few inches taller than Jeremy's six-foot-one, with a leaner body and a sensual stride that gave both men and women whiplash when he walked by. They either wanted to be him or be with him, but no one could ignore him.

Least of all Jeremy. His body reacted instantly to the scenery and he sighed, knowing it was going to be a long night.

Getting hard at the sight of Owen was nothing new. Jeremy had known ever since they met that being friends with him would mean a lot of cold showers.

He was a damn handsome man, though too much of an alpha male and too much like Jeremy to be his usual type, even if he had been open to it. Still, he'd always been a temptation. The unattainable usually was.

Owen snapped his fingers in Jeremy's face. "Earth to Porter. Thinking of ways to get our favorite vigilante demon out of his current dilemma, or were you staring at my ass?"

"Fuck off," Jeremy blustered, turning toward the living room, pizza box still in hand. "Just for that you'll have to wait for this edition to hit the stands."

"Bullshit. You never make me wait for it. It's one of

the things I like best about you."

Damn, the way he'd said that sounded sexy.

"That, and your big screen."

And *that* sounded like Owen.

He *had* been staring, and Owen knew it. Jeremy had never seen the need to hide his bisexuality from his best friend, though he didn't throw it in his face either. Finn was a man's man from a traditional Irish family. He loved sports, worked with his hands and hadn't lacked for female companionship since he hit puberty. In other words, he was arrow straight.

Maybe straight wasn't the right word for him, Jeremy thought as he set the box on the coffee table. Owen had more than a few kinks from, what he'd been told, and he was a bit of a player with the ladies, but sex with other men had never been on his agenda.

They didn't talk much about their individual predilections with each other. Owen knew Jeremy liked men as well as women, and Jeremy knew Owen frequented the same BDSM club that their friend Tasha was a member of. It didn't have anything to do with their friendship.

Or it hadn't until Tasha's party.

He walked over to the fifty-inch flat screen framed by

shelves of movies and games. "Sports or swords?"

"Swords," Owen responded as he threw himself onto the wide leather couch and opened his beer. "I had a long day, and I'm in the mood for a bloody birthday massacre."

"Should I ask?"

"God, no."

Jeremy slipped the game into the console and tossed the two controllers on the couch beside his friend. "It's your birthday. And there will be blood."

"Blood and pizza. It doesn't get better."

They spent the next hour swapping smack talk and grabbing bites of pizza between battles. Jeremy leaned back on the couch, his fingers automatically controlling his character's movements as his mind drifted.

This was it then—business as usual. Fine. It was better this way. Their friendship was intact. He wouldn't have to think about his own reactions to the incident at Tasha's party, or how he'd wished it had been Owen he was with that night instead of the man whose name he hadn't bothered to remember.

Natasha Rivera had introduced him to the stranger. She was the only friend from high school besides Owen that he was still close to. The three of them had been through a lot together, though their individual relationships with Jeremy couldn't be more different. Both a voyeur and an exhibitionist, Tasha was also Jeremy's occasional lover, and that evening she'd had her heart set on watching him fuck another man. One of her favorite requests.

Tasha's choice for their third, a pretty and unabashedly gay coworker, had shown a flattering fascination with the fit of Jeremy's jeans and Tasha's hints about what they were hiding. Against his better judgment, Jeremy had let the two of them drag him into the bedroom and strip off his clothes during the party instead of making them wait until it was over. He'd let them caress his body and measure the length of his erection with their hands, though he could hear the beat of the bass and the murmur of the crowd from the other room.

They'd both knelt at his feet and taken turns sucking on his cock, until eventually he'd stopped trying to remember if they'd locked the door and let his desire take over. He'd been so aroused and distracted by their joint effort he ended up bending that hot twenty-something blond over the bed, sliding on a condom and giving him the fucking he'd been vocally begging for.

That was how Owen found them when he walked in. He'd frozen—a tall, still shadow framed in light and loud music.

Jeremy had been startled too, but when he realized who was in the doorway and what Owen was seeing—him with his pants around his ankles and his dick disappearing into another man's ass, the voluptuous, caramel-skinned Tasha naked and touching herself beside them as she watched—some inner devil loosed by drink and lust had taken over his body.

He hadn't stopped. In fact, he'd taken hold of his partner's shoulder and started slamming into him so hard he was worried the bed or the lean body beneath him would break. And he hadn't taken his eyes off Owen.

"Fuck," the man had gasped. "*Fuck, yeah*. Oh God, give it to me. Pound my ass with that big fat cock!"

Owen had flinched at the graphic demand, his gaze clashing with Jeremy's for a few devastating heartbeats before he backed out of the room and closed the door.

Turned on as hell, Jeremy had ridden Tasha's screaming morsel of a coworker without mercy, imagining it was Owen he was fucking instead. Then he'd buried his face between Tasha's thighs and made her come so violently she swore she saw stars. By the time he finished and came out to look for his friend, Owen had already left the party and Jeremy's satisfaction had swiftly turned into regret.

"He's a big boy, honey," Tasha had assured him later, when everyone else had gone and they were sharing the last of a bottle of Scotch. "He knows you and I like variety. He does too. *He's* plowed through so many women in the last year you'd think he was going for a record. Even his brothers have pulled him aside and told him to turn it down a notch."

"It's not the same thing."

"It is exactly the same thing. We are consenting adults having a little harmless fun. You should see what Master Finn does to his partners at the club." She lifted the finely arched eyebrows over her sparkling green eyes. "You'd blush, but none of those little submissives can resist him. Hell, most of the Doms have a difficult time."

"Yet you do."

She'd looked away from him, the way she always did when the subject came up. "I resist all Finns. Especially the ones who seem to be working out their personal demons on every warm body that isn't nailed down."

Owen's demons and laundry list of conquests aside,

Jeremy couldn't help but feel the sting of his own shame. Not because Owen had seen them, but because of how he'd felt knowing his oldest, closest and most profoundly heterosexual friend had watched him in action.

It had turned him on. Hell, it was turning him on right now. What the hell kind of a person did that make him?

Owen's laugh interrupted his morose thoughts. "You are really off your game tonight, aren't you? Your undefeated champion just got his head lopped off by a tree-dwelling ogre and you didn't even notice."

"Sorry." Jeremy shifted, his controller doing little to hide his erection. He pressed the pause button on the game. "Another beer?"

Though Owen was looking at him with a curious expression, he nodded. "Yeah, thanks."

Jeremy got up and walked swiftly to the kitchen. He needed to get this reaction reined in. This man's friendship was the most important thing in his life. He could be a stubborn jackass, but he was loyal and dedicated to the people he cared about. And his family— the Finns had always been there for him. Even when no one else was. A fact he tried to remember to help control his desire to jump their son.

He was holding the neck of a cold bottle when he turned to find Owen leaning against the counter across from him, arms folded. "Did you want something else instead? Coffee? I have tequila."

"Tequila sounds good." His subdued smile made Jeremy wary.

"I feel guilty as hell that I didn't have time to get you a cake." Jeremy grabbed two shot glasses and filled them, handing one to Owen before tapping their glasses together. "But maybe this will do instead. Happy Birthday, man."

"I don't want cake." Owen threw back his shot and slowly lowered his glass, licking the remnants from his lips. "This works just fine."

Jeremy followed suit, feeling the heat hit his stomach and spread through his limbs. He lifted the bottle and studied the contents, hoping it would be enough to get his mind off of Owen's lips. "Another?"

He shook his head. "That might not be a good idea. The guys at work made me down a few shots already. Probably to prepare me for my present."

"What did they get you?"

"A stripper. They actually brought her to my office."

"To that shitty-ass trailer?" Jeremy tried to smile

back. "Sounds like somebody wants a raise."

"My money is on Scott, but he's not getting one. It wasn't exactly a professional thing to do."

"Says the man who almost convinced a chorus line of topless dancers to attend our college graduation ceremony," Jeremy said dryly. "If it *was* him, he has to at least get points for showing initiative. That would be more work than he's done all year."

When Owen didn't respond, he raised his brows in question. "Well don't keep me in suspense. How was she?"

"I was bored." He heard the thread of disbelief in Owen's voice. "She was hot and naked and her breasts were…" He made a gesture with his hands to indicate their size. "She was really working for it too, grinding on my lap with an impressive amount of skill. But I was bored and it showed. I had to think about something else and give her a big tip just so she wouldn't be insulted."

Jeremy whistled, reaching for his beer bottle and stepping back to lean against the refrigerator. "I didn't realize thirty-five was the cutoff date for the sex drive. Sounds like I only have three months left to enjoy myself. I'll stock up on energy drinks right away and clear my schedule."

"Fuck off, Porter." Owen glared. "I have no problems with my sex drive. My mind was on other things."

"Your drive is well known, buddy, which is why I'm surprised. What could occupy sexual legend Owen Finn's mind so much that a naked woman on your lap couldn't tempt you?"

"It happens." Owen tilted his head, as if considering his words, but Jeremy saw his eyes drop to the bulge in his jeans. Damn it, he was hoping he wouldn't notice. "But obviously not to you. If Natasha's hype is to be believed, you're the legend."

Jeremy snorted in denial, but Owen wasn't deterred. "She's been telling me stories about your sexual adventures for a while but I never paid much attention. To be honest, when it started I thought she was making it up so I would stop asking her out. Maybe she thought I'd have a problem sleeping with my best friend's fuck buddy. Maybe she thought I'd be intimidated by the sheer number of times you've convinced two people to sleep with you at once."

"She knows you better than that. You love a challenge." Jeremy sighed, pressing his back against the door of his fridge and tightening his fingers around his beer bottle. Of course the topic occupying Owen's mind was Tasha, not him. He should have known it would be. Just like Jeremy, Owen wanted what he couldn't have. "And I don't have any claim on her, not like that. But she does like her stories. I've heard a few about you too. She likes to wind us up. Does her best to shock me."

"No shit?" His friend shifted, his brow furrowing a little at that. "What does she say about *me* that's so shocking?"

"True torture chamber stuff. And her delivery is what really sells it. All that's missing is a campfire and marshmallows."

His blue eyes had narrowed. "So she talks about what I do at the club? With you?"

"It's Tasha, man," Jeremy reassured him softly. "And it's me. Don't get all 'What happens in Fight Club' on me. I'm not judging."

"*Torture chamber stuff* sounds like judging. You shouldn't knock it until you've tried it." Owen paused. "Have you? Any of your threesomes gone beyond the usual bedroom play? Anyone want to tie you up or spank you? Don't tell me Tasha's never asked."

This was not the right conversation to get his mind off of sex. "She hasn't, and neither has anyone else. No one would dare. You're both aware that's not my thing, but you know my motto. Whatever turns you on is good by me."

"That was mine until a few weeks ago," Owen muttered.

Damn it.

"So we *are* going to talk about it." Jeremy tried to play it nonchalant, feeling anything but. "This is me, officially apologizing. We should've locked the door, I know. But I don't think we scarred you for life, did we? I mean, you chain women to crosses and mark them up with a tool chest full of kink for fun. All I do is—"

"Fuck men while Tasha watches."

Jeremy ran a hand through his hair. "Yeah, well, I do that when she doesn't watch too. I also fuck other women on occasion. I've got an equal-opportunity dick. It takes all comers."

"Funny."

He narrowed his gaze on Owen. "If I crossed a line with Natasha without knowing it, if you're planning on seriously pursuing her, I'll back off. I'm not trying to take anything from you. You know I would never do that."

Owen shook his head, an expression of frustration crossing his handsome face. "No. I mean, yes, it's never been a secret that I wanted her. Everybody wants her. Even you. Hell, even my brothers—well, you'd have to be a eunuch not to. But she has her own play partners and no interest in dating me. She knows her own mind, and the last thing I'd ever do is warn you away. She'd kick my ass or get her grandmother in Puerto Rico to curse my manhood—which is a threat she's used on me more than once. Believe it or not, she isn't the problem."

Now Jeremy was confused. He'd been so sure he was right. "You can tell me the truth. It's obvious seeing her with me rattled you. If you ask my opinion, I think you could win her over if you—"

"Just stop," Owen bit out forcefully. "This isn't about her, damn it. It's about *you*."

Jeremy's head jerked back in surprise. "Me? What about me?"

"Hell." Owen swallowed, his blue eyes going dark. "You're going to make me spell it out. Fine."

He took a step toward Jeremy, yanking the beer out of his hand and setting it on the counter.

"Owen, what the fuck?"

He was standing so close Jeremy could feel his body heat, feel his breath on his cheek as he spoke. "You want to know what I was thinking about today? What got me hard while my birthday present was jiggling her giant tits in my face? That night. I haven't been able to stop thinking about the three of you in that room."

"Is that what's been bothering you? Seriously? That's…that's normal, Owen," Jeremy assured him softly, trying not to show any outward reaction to his words. "No man's dick is immune to a live porn show. Threesomes are hot and we're visual creatures. It's the nature of the beast. It doesn't have to mean anything."

"Trying to reassure the nervous heterosexual?" Owen chuckled roughly. "That's sweet. Is it normal that Tasha was nearly naked with her legs spread invitingly, but *you* were the one I couldn't stop looking at? That I keep hearing what that guy said about you when you…"

His words faded and he backed away enough to take another look at Jeremy's now snug jeans. "Did you like it? Having him beg for you like that? Is that why you didn't stop when you saw me?"

"Owen…"

"I should have turned around the second I opened the door, but I didn't. Not even when I knew you could see me." He looked up suddenly, his blue eyes pinning Jeremy in place. "Did you like knowing I was there? Because for a second there, I could have sworn you did."

Sweet Jesus. "Why are we talking about this?"

"We talk about everything else, Jeremy. Why not this?"

"We never do." He took a drink and tried to calm his nerves. "We don't compare stories about our conquests. We don't talk about sex."

Because you don't want to hear about what I do, and I don't need any more fodder for my fantasies.

"I think it's time we changed that rule, and I'll start. I have a request. Call it a birthday present. You do still owe me one, and as you said, you didn't even get me a cake." Owen paused and Jeremy felt his stomach knot. "I'd like to see it."

"See what?" But he knew. He'd never witnessed that expression on Owen's face. It was sensual. Mesmerizing. Commanding.

"Your cock. I want to see it for myself. I've never been this interested before." Owen shifted, looking rueful. "Well, that's not entirely true. I've actually been thinking about it for a while now."

"You have?" Did his voice sound unusually high? It did to him.

Owen tilted his head. "You could help me. I've been asked to top men at the club and I always hesitate—not because I'm a homophobe, but because I wasn't sure I could give them what they needed. But you know what men need, don't you?"

Jeremy couldn't stop staring. Owen wanted to see his cock? So he could learn how to give *other guys* what they wanted?

"Sorry," he finally said, "but I can't help you with that, Owen. I'm not going to whip out my dick for your fetish research."

Owen licked his lips. "Fine. Not research then. We can call it intense personal curiosity. A favor from one friend to another. We've done favors for each other before. To make it fair..." He smiled and Jeremy knew he was in trouble. "I'll show you mine if you show me yours."

CHAPTER TWO

Jeremy tried to laugh but his throat was too tight. This wasn't happening. "Are you yanking my chain? I know, this wouldn't be the first time but this is hardcore, even for you. Are you *that* upset by what happened at the party?"

"I'm not upset but I am serious." Owen's hands went to his belt and unbuckled it. "Show me," he dared in a soft, deep voice that Jeremy couldn't help but respond to.

Oh holy fuck.

Jeremy's hands went to the top button on his jeans, almost without conscious thought. He kept his eyes on Owen's as he lowered the zipper over his swiftly hardening erection, waiting to be stopped.

Owen didn't stop him.

"This is some fucked-up slumber party shit, Finn," he told him roughly. "Should we get out the measuring sticks?"

Owen's attention was focused on the bulge still covered by denim. "This is *my* slumber party. Take it out, Jeremy. Let me see it."

He was really doing this. Jesus, he was so turned on his teeth ground together when he gripped his painfully hard shaft, pulling it out of his jeans right there in the kitchen. Right in front of Owen Finn.

Owen's hands paused on his own zipper and he moved in for a closer look. Was that flush blooming on his cheeks from arousal? "Damn. He wasn't lying, was he? That is one big, fat cock. I think I might be jealous. No wonder they beg for it."

Oh God. "There. Now you've seen it. Let's stop pretending we're twelve and have another drink." He started to force it back into his jeans but Owen shook his head.

"Wait." He licked his lips and Jeremy's knees nearly buckled. "We had an agreement. I'm supposed to show you mine."

He parted his jeans and pulled himself out, and just

22

like that, Jeremy felt like begging. How many times had he thought about it? Wondered how it would look? Feel?

"Well?"

"It's good." Fuck, it was so good and already hard. Not as long as his—not many were—but thick and totally aroused. "Real good, man. You should be proud. Are we done?"

Owen chuckled. "Am I making you uncomfortable, Mr. Threesome?"

He shook his head but admitted, "I'm not quite drunk enough to find this game as amusing as you seem to."

"This isn't a game. And turned on would be more accurate. So hard I hurt would be closer to the truth. Can I touch you?"

He inhaled sharply, too shocked to move away when Owen leaned forward and brushed his lips across Jeremy's, both of them still holding their erections in their hands.

"God, that's weird. That's the first time I've been scratched by a beard," Owen muttered. "Sorry, I couldn't resist. Can I touch you?" he repeated.

Yes. Please. No...Oh God. "I don't know what you're trying to do here, but I really don't think you've thought this through."

"You want me to. You *really* want it. Or is your dick so equal-opportunity that any breeze will do?"

"You know you're drunk." Jeremy pushed out the accusation breathlessly, so turned on he was afraid he might come right there in front of him. "You said they gave you shots at work. Or maybe the mushrooms on the damn pizza were off. Damn it, Owen, this isn't you."

"I didn't think it was me either, believe me. I tried to remember that every day for two weeks. I wore out my little black book trying to fuck away the image of you making that stranger crazy enough to beg. I visited the club every day for a week and it wasn't enough. I still replayed it in my mind at night when I closed my eyes, until I got so hard I had to jerk off before I could sleep."

He reached for Jeremy's free hand and placed it on his flat stomach, under his t-shirt and just above his erection. He was so warm. "You can touch me too if you want, but I need you to give me permission to do the same. I'm tired of wondering, Jeremy. You know better than anyone how I am when I get an idea in my head. I can't get this one out until I know. Don't tell me you've never been curious about what it would be like to do this. I know you've thought about it. I saw it in your eyes that night. And you've been hard since I got here."

"Owen, *you* need to think about it," Jeremy begged, even as his hand slid down the hard abs he'd longed to touch and his fingers brushed the head of Owen's erection. *Finally. Yes.* "Think about what happens tomorrow."

Owen let out a shaky breath. "I don't want to think anymore. Jesus, your hand is hot. I've never had another man touch me like this, Jeremy. Never wanted them to. Just touch it. Tell me I can repay the favor. Say yes."

It came out before he could stop it. "Yes."

Jeremy moaned when Owen wrapped his long, work-roughened fingers around his shaft. "Jesus, that's a monster," he heard him breathe. "I'm not surprised he was screaming for more."

There was only so much he could take. How many times had he imagined having Owen willing? Touching him, feeling him in his hands... Fuck, he'd wanted it for so long.

Owen moaned in surprise and desire as Jeremy tightened his fingers around him and skillfully stroked his length, leaning in to take control of the next kiss and forcing open willing lips with his tongue.

Yes. Kissing Owen. Touching Owen.

The hand on Jeremy's dick was trembling, and he

reminded himself that Owen didn't know what he was asking for. He was experimenting. Testing uncharted waters.

Stroking his erection.

Owen was the one who tore his lips away first. "You're good at that. I should have known you would be. And that mouth. I bet they beg for your mouth too, don't they?"

His thoughts were torn in two different directions.

Have to stay in control. Have to give him more.

Jeremy wrapped his free arm around him, in one rough move reversing their positions so Owen was the one with his back pressed against the cold steel door. He looked Owen in the eye, held his gaze for a heartbeat, then dropped to his knees and roughly shucked Owen's pants down to the tops of his thighs.

"*Yes*, Jeremy."

After another heartbeat to catch his breath at the sight of the thick erection in front of him, he took it into his mouth, closing his eyes as he got his first taste. Jesus, he could come from this alone. Owen's hard cock filling his mouth. Owen moaning his name.

Owen.

"*Fuck*. Jesus, you didn't have to…" Owen's voice

trailed off and Jeremy felt his strong, calloused fingers tangle and snag in his hair. "*Damn*. Damn, that's good. You don't know how many times I imagined this, but it's better."

Jeremy knew it was. He'd learned a long time ago that most men were good at sucking cock. Straight, gay or bi, men knew what they liked. But he was a master. With his size, he'd had to be. He'd had to learn to drive a man crazy enough that they'd be willing to take him. Begging to take him. He knew exactly how hard he could suck, knew how much Owen would love to feel his throat tighten around his shaft as he swallowed. Knew what to do with his tongue and how firmly he could grip the base with his fingers so the tension would build and intensify.

Owen's hands clenched harder in his hair and his hips thrust forward helplessly. "Now I *am* jealous," he rasped, obviously struggling for control. "Or grateful for all the practice you had to get this good. *Fuck*. Fuck it's so good. I can't—"

Owen made a strangled sound and Jeremy took a breath and relaxed his throat, knowing what he needed. He lifted both his hands to Owen's hips when they started pumping, taking in more of the thick girth as

Owen thrust his way to climax between his lips.

Yes. Let me taste you, baby. Fuck my mouth. Gonna make you come so hard you'll never forget.

Jeremy heard the shout and tasted salt and man and as Owen's release filled his mouth. He swallowed it with a deep groan, greedy for every drop, for every second that it lasted. He was overwhelmed by the flavor, the scent, and how lost Owen seemed in climax. He reveled in the feeling of the shaft pulsing inside his mouth, the power of having this strong body tremble with the pleasure Jeremy had given him.

So good, baby. You taste so good.

"And that answers *that* question," Owen gasped, still panting from his orgasm.

Owen. Jesus, this was his friend, not some drunken stranger.

Jeremy pulled up Owen's jeans, got to his feet unsteadily and turned, walking out of the kitchen without a word. That hadn't just happened. He hadn't just dropped to his knees and ruined in five minutes what he'd built up over nineteen years.

"Where are you going? What the hell? Jeremy, stop."

Owen grabbed his arm just as he reached the living room and he snapped. Before he could protest Jeremy had him bent over the couch with one hand pressed behind his back and his body hard against him.

"What?" Jeremy growled, dragging Owen's jeans back down just enough to feel the bare skin of his ass against his aching erection. "Still curious? Want some more show and tell?"

He rocked himself between the firm cheeks of Owen's ass, unable to hold back his moan. It felt too good. "Don't try and top me, Owen. You would be running if you knew what usually happens next in this scenario. A few drinks and a blatant invitation like that? Any other man would forget the consequences and bury himself balls deep inside your virgin ass. But that's not what I'm going to do."

"Fine." Owen bucked against him in challenge, but not hard enough to get free. "Give me a minute to recover and I can fuck you instead."

Jeremy's laugh was humorless. "That's not how this works, buddy." He released him and straightened, his hands clenched in fists at his sides to still their shaking as he watched Owen stand and pull up his pants. "I don't catch, and from what I hear, it wouldn't be your style either, *Master* Finn. Since I'm not into collars and you're not into dicks, just take your birthday blowjob and go. If we both have a few more drinks before bed we can chalk this up to temporary insanity between old friends. I will take it to my grave if you do the same. No one else ever has to know."

Jeremy crawled over the back of his couch and sat down, one arm covering his eyes as he waited to hear the sounds of Owen leaving. God, he wanted him to stay. He wanted to suck Owen's dick into his mouth and work it until it was hard again. Wanted to spread the cheeks of his ass and fuck it with his tongue and fingers. Anything so he could hear more of those sexy sounds of surprised pleasure Owen had made.

The real birthday surprise was on him. Owen liked what Jeremy had done to him. He'd initiated it. It only made the situation—and his cock—harder.

They must have given Owen more to drink at work than he was admitting to. Or they'd slipped something in it. Maybe he should call him a cab. Take him to the hospital to get checked out.

The sound of the coffee table sliding across his wood floor made Jeremy lift his arm and open his eyes. Owen had kicked it out of the way so he could stand in front of him. "Fuck, man, what now?"

Owen bent over him, a determined smile on his lips.

He gripped the open waistband of Jeremy's jeans and abruptly yanked them down to his ankles, practically lifting his hips off the couch in the process.

"Owen, shit!"

"You have this mistaken impression that you scared me off with your Tarzan routine and we're done with my birthday party. But if you want me to slink away and act like this never happened tomorrow—if we're taking this to our graves—I may as well satisfy all my curiosity tonight."

He spread Jeremy's thighs and knelt between them, licking his lips and looking up at him with lust in his eyes. "I've never done this before either, and *that's* something I haven't said in years. You're going to have to tell me what you like."

"*Jesus fucking Christ, Owen,*" Jeremy moaned when he watched the blond head dip over his erection. How could he say no to that? To everything he ever wanted right in front of him? Not even a saint would have the strength, and God knew he was no saint.

He felt lips wrap hesitantly around the head of his shaft and he ran his fingers gently over Owen's head. "Stubborn jackass. Just take what you can. *Ah, God.* I'll like whatever you do."

Owen's tongue traced a vein on his shaft and Jeremy shuddered. It was like waking up in a damn dream, watching that mouth explore his cock. Owen was slow but thorough, taking his time to learn every inch of him with his lips and tongue before he started sucking lightly.

Too lightly.

"Fuck," Jeremy swore, forgetting his earlier praise as lust began to consume him. "I need more than that, Owen. I'm hard not fragile. It's not going to break if you suck it like you want it."

Owen groaned and sucked harder, trying to take more. Jeremy felt the tug all the way up his damn spine and watched those lips stretch around him with sensual satisfaction. He cupped the back of Owen's head, holding him there. "*Yes*. Yeah, that's it. You're a natural."

Oh God, he was going to Hell. He should stop him. He shouldn't be lifting his hips in a plea for more, shouldn't be loving the sight of Owen struggling to swallow him whole, tears leaking from his eyes as it hit the back of his throat. And still, Owen couldn't take it all.

"Damn, that's nice." Better than nice. It might kill

him.

He tensed when Owen pulled away from his touch, lifting his mouth to stare at him for one silent, tense moment. His eyes sparkled when he slipped his middle finger in his mouth and then lowered it between Jeremy's legs.

Oh hell. "What do you think you're doing?"

"I bet you can guess."

"Damn it, Owen, I told you I don't catch."

"Let me. Just once and I'll make you come. Let me show you what I can do."

"Fuck."

"I'll take that as a yes. And don't worry," Owen assured him gruffly. "I'm a natural."

He couldn't restrain his shout of surprise when Owen wrapped his lips around his cock again as his wet finger slipped between the cheeks of his ass and pushed inside.

"*Owen*. That feels… Oh, *fuck*."

Yes! Stick it in deeper. Fuck me, Owen. So good.

Jeremy was helpless, his hips rising and falling, caught between the thrusts of Owen's finger and his hot, talented mouth. Owen's mouth on him. Owen's finger inside his ass. The taste of him still on his tongue. He couldn't think of anything else. Couldn't hold back. "I'm close."

Owen grunted against his shaft and sucked so hard his cheeks hollowed. The sensation rang him like a fucking bell. Jeremy wasn't going to last. He tugged on the soft blond hair in his hands, knowing what would happen next. "I have to come, damn it. If you don't want—Christ!"

Owen's finger thrust deep and pressed against a spot that made Jeremy's body arch off the couch as he came. He was on fire, every nerve raw and shooting off sparks.

Coming so hard in your mouth, baby. Coming for you. Take it all.

Owen choked but didn't lift his head, giving as good as he'd gotten. It drove Jeremy wild even as he shook with the force of his climax and the knowledge of who had given it to him.

"Oh hell yeah," he murmured, caressing Owen's cheek as the man licked his shaft. Definitely a natural.

Jeremy held his breath when he realized Owen was studying him again. His cheeks were flushed, his lips swollen and shimmering with Jeremy's release. He'd never seen him like this. Aroused. Sensual. It was sexy as hell.

"See? I knew you'd like that." Owen's voice was

deep. Determined. "So do I. And I know I could get better with a little practice."

"Trust me, you don't need to get any better."

"I'm a competitive man."

"We're even. Let's call it even."

He nodded, his lips quirking in a sideways smile. "Fine. But we're still not done."

Sexy as hell and stubborn as a mule.

"Owen, man, think about this." Even as he said the words again Jeremy shivered with an aftershock of pleasure.

He wants more.

"You keep saying that. I have. I told you. You can be worried about tomorrow, but I'm not. We've known each other a long damn time. Been friends a long damn time. This isn't going to change that."

Was he really that naïve? "This always changes things."

Owen frowned. "Fine. Then we'll deal with it. But not tonight."

He stood and held out his hand without another word. Jeremy hesitated. He wanted more too. He wanted everything, but there were some things he wouldn't let Owen tempt him into. Some things there could be no coming back from. But he could have him. Just for one night, he could have more of him.

Owen wanted it. Was asking for it. And no one else would ever know.

Sucking his cock had made Owen hard again.

Jeremy stood beside him, stepping out of his pants and letting himself be led down the hall to the bedroom.

He couldn't say no.

CHAPTER THREE

They were naked in the shower, in *his* shower, kissing and exploring each other's bodies with a sensual curiosity that drove Jeremy wild. He stroked the smooth, lean muscles he'd longed to touch for years. Owen felt even better than he'd always looked. Stronger. And the firm, rough feel of his calloused hands on Jeremy's body was hotter than his dirtiest dream.

So much better it scared him.

Owen drew back with a deep chuckle that echoed off the tile walls. "I'm sorry, but you're killing me, man. How attached are you to that beard?"

"My beard?" Pulling out of his lust-induced haze with difficulty, Jeremy raised one hand to scratch at his furry jaw, frowning distractedly. "It's pretty attached to

37

me. Why?"

The wicked smile that spread across Owen's face was so confident it made Jeremy's throat tighten. "Shave it off."

What?

"Hell no, Finn. I've been growing this out for nearly two years."

"I know," Owen replied wryly. "And you grow a good beard, I'll give you that. But I want you to shave it off now."

"Now? You want me to stop what we're doing and shave *right now*?" Jeremy started to laugh until he realized he was serious.

"I do." Owen opened the shower door. "I'll watch."

"Why?"

Owen shrugged. "It's been a while since I've seen your face, for one. And I don't want to have to explain away a body covered in beard burn tomorrow."

Jeremy couldn't believe he was considering it. "You expect me to shave this beauty off for one night of satisfying your curiosity? You really think you're worth that kind of sacrifice?"

"I know I am. And so do you. I've got plans for that mouth, Jeremy." Owen bit his lower lip seductively and his palm slid over Jeremy's hip, making him groan. "Come on. The beard will grow back. You don't want to stop kissing me, do you?"

Oh, that was low. And effective.

Bastard.

Jeremy huffed, but walked out of the shower and stood soaking on the mat while he reached for his scissors and electric razor. He felt the need to register some sort of protest, even as he lifted the scissors to his dark beard and watched the hair fall into the sink.

"Tasha likes my beard. Says it makes her thighs tingle for days after. Come to think of it, no one else has had any complaints."

"Tasha likes your big, equal-opportunity dick," Owen laughed, letting the water spray against his back as he watched Jeremy. "She also has a higher threshold for pain than I do. She's switched once or twice, and I've seen her played."

"So you can dish it out but you can't take it? From what I hear, you're a rough son of a bitch."

Jeremy sent him a look that was meant to be teasing, but then he stilled, unable to look away. Owen was slowly stroking his erection as he stared at Jeremy's body. Goddamn, he was sexy.

Irresistibly drawn, Jeremy started to move back toward him.

"Keep trimming if you want me to respond to that," Owen ordered. "I can be rough, if that's what it takes to bring my partner pleasure. And I admit I get off on it. Seeing that look of bliss they get when they let go of everything else and just feel. Most of them are a lot like you, you know."

"Men?" Jeremy tried to joke but he was having a hard time breathing.

Owen shook his head patiently. "Responsible. Controlled. Repressed."

"Hello? I'm an openly, *actively* bisexual artist. I'm covered in tattoos, in touch with my inner child and the life of every damn party. I'm hardly repressed. I'm the poster boy for freedom of expression."

"A poster boy with an impressive stick up your ass and a castle moat around your emotions. I think tonight is the first time I've seen you really let go. From where I'm standing, you're all bottled up and ready to pop. Giving up control could be just what you need."

"No way." Jeremy's voice was higher than he wanted it to be. Excited. "You may be curious but I'm not. Not about your kind of play, Finn. I'm pretty sure a guy hits

40

me? I'll hit him right back."

"You might surprise yourself. Why don't you look back in the mirror and concentrate for me?"

He waited in silence until Jeremy forced himself to do as he asked.

When he started talking again, Jeremy could hear the approval in his voice. "Good. We can get into that later. Right now I want to know what it's like to kiss you without that beard. To bite your chin. I want to touch your smooth face, those tattoos on your back, and the ones on your thighs and ass that you got in New Zealand last year. Who did you say did them?"

Jeremy steadied his hand as he trimmed the beard as close as he could get it, trying to focus on the question. "One of my Maori friends from the convention took me to his cousin. It seemed like a good idea at the time."

"It was," Owen assured him. "I mean you told me you had some new ink, but I had no idea. You look like a different person without your clothes on. That workout room has really paid off too. You're big. Everywhere. Primitive, powerful and intimidating as fuck. I can see you chasing someone down and pinning them to the ground, pulling their hair while you fuck them. I thought about it as soon as you bent me over the couch. There's a kink for that you know—it's not one I've explored, but I could get interested in it now."

Who was this sexual stranger who'd taken over his best friend's body? The things he was saying... Jeremy knew without looking that Owen was still touching himself. "Do you want me to cut myself and bleed out? Is that your goal here?"

"Am I distracting you?" Owen laughed.

"Just stop talking." He turned on the razor and focused on shaving. The remnants of his black and gray beard disappeared and Jeremy felt as if he were going back in time.

He had a sudden flashback of all the nights he'd spent over at Owen's house when his aunt was on a bender. Those times he'd lain in his sleeping bag on the floor next to his friend's bed, waiting for him to fall asleep. By the time he turned seventeen he hadn't been able to resist thinking about Owen and what they could be like together. He'd held his breath and bitten his cheek as hard as he could to silence his sounds of pleasure while he stroked himself to climax in the dark room.

Maybe he was still dreaming, because the Owen from his fantasies was here, ready to let Jeremy do whatever he wanted to his body. It was too good to be true. Impossible to believe. Another shoe was bound to fall and hit him right between the eyes, forcing him to wake up.

He rinsed and wiped off his face when he was done, noticing how odd the cool air felt on his bare cheeks. The man in the mirror was unrecognizable. More vulnerable, despite his size. He turned back toward Owen with his jaw and chin on display. "Satisfied I won't damage your sensitive skin now?"

Owen's chest was rising and falling rapidly, his knuckles white as he gripped the base of his shaft. "I forgot you had dimples. You look like a new man."

Jeremy stalked his way back to the shower, digging his fingers into Owen's arms and walking him backward until his back was flush with the tile. "Let's test out the new me."

He kissed him so there could be no mistaking his intent, and they both moaned as their bodies rubbed against each other. Owen's fingers brushed Jeremy's erection and then he wrapped both hands around it, rubbing it against his own.

Jeremy swore and ground his hips against him, loving the slide of their wet skin. He bit Owen's lower lip and he felt him shiver. The man who loved to dominate wanted to be pinned down and fucked. Wanted to be bitten.

He did it again.

Owen turned his head, breaking the kiss. "Suck me off again," he demanded roughly. "I want to know if it feels as good without the beard."

Jeremy shook his head, knowing his demand was as much a battle of wills as it was a desire. "I don't think so. Not yet."

He turned Owen around facing the narrow bench he'd had installed and put a strong hand between his shoulder blades. "Bend over."

Owen tensed and Jeremy placed an open mouthed kiss on his shoulder. "I'm just going to give you back a little bit of what you gave me in the living room. Just want to touch you."

Relaxing at Jeremy's reassurance, Owen bent over, spreading his legs for balance and placing his hands on the bench. "That finger trick? I had a woman do that to me once in the middle of the deed. Surprised the hell out of me. I swear when I came I thought, 'Well no fucking wonder Jeremy likes this.' Of course, then I had to spank her and return the favor."

Jeremy smiled grimly and hesitated before reaching for the bottle of lube. Owen expected it now. Was waiting for it. He was too comfortable, and it made Jeremy want to do something unexpected. "Now that I'm newly shaved, I think I want to try something else first."

He spread the cheeks of Owen's ass with his thumbs, not waiting for a reply before he dipped down and licked the tight ring of muscles he was dying to fuck with his tongue.

"Jeremy?" Owen's voice was soft. Stunned. "Are you—*oh, God.*"

Hell, yes. Jeremy squeezed the flesh in his hands as he flicked his tongue over the sensitive skin, loving Owen's surprised groans and the way his hips tilted instinctively—unconsciously begging for more.

Jeremy wanted to give it to him. He pushed his tongue inside and was rewarded with a shout that echoed off the bathroom walls.

"Fuck!"

You like that, Master Finn? Like having a man fucking rim your ass and make you beg?

"Jeremy!" Owen was rocking helplessly against Jeremy's mouth. "Jesus, I didn't know it would feel like that. I've never..."

Jeremy could feel how much he liked it. Hear it in the sounds he was making. Owen may be new to the game but he was a fast learner. So fast it was hard for Jeremy to remember he needed to take it slow.

"Fuck," Owen was muttering. "It shouldn't be this good. Why is it so good? *Yes*. Deeper."

Jeremy thrust his tongue deep once, twice, then lifted his mouth and grabbed for the lube he kept in the shower for special occasions. He tipped it over and watched the thick liquid run between Owen's cheeks.

Owen was swearing, his body practically vibrating with desire. "Why did you stop?"

"Just trying to give you what you want, Owen." His moved, his erection pressed against Owen's hip as his fingers caressed him. "You said you needed it deeper."

Gripping Owen's cock with his free hand, Jeremy pushed one long finger inside his ass.

"Fuck, you're tight," he groaned when Owen let out a ragged breath. He pushed in, massaging him in a way he knew would drive him crazy. "Talk to me now, Owen. Tell me you like your birthday present. That you're enjoying your little walk on the wild side."

Owen was shaking against him as Jeremy stroked his

cock in time to the slow thrusts of his finger. "Jeremy I—*yes*."

"That's all you're going to give me?" Jeremy made a tsking sound. "Monosyllabic man-speak doesn't work for me. Should I stop and try something else?"

Owen's voice was a study in frustration. "I fucking *love* it, okay? Don't stop."

"You love what?"

"Everything. It all feels good. What you're doing now. Your tongue. Jesus, I didn't know I would want something like that, Jeremy. That it would blow my damn mind. Is that what you want to hear?"

Jeremy bit him hard on the shoulder. "I did shave for you. A little positive feedback isn't too much to ask."

"Fuck you," Owen moaned. "Or me. Jesus, fuck *me*, Jeremy. I can take whatever you can dish out."

Jeremy's body jerked at that and he swore. "You don't know what you're talking about. But let me give you a hint." He pulled out, then added a second finger to the first, gritting his teeth at the slow insertion and the snug fit.

Owen let out a shout and slammed his hand down on the bench. "Too much. That's too much. I can't—"

"*That's* what you're asking for, Owen. That and

more. You think it's too much now?" Jeremy rubbed his prostrate with the tips of his fingers, unable to stop himself from soothing the pressure, unable to deny his pleasure when Owen cried his name again. "You wouldn't be able to take me with an ass this tight."

"Holy shit, how are you doing that? *Mother fucker!*"

"You like that?"

"Yes, damn you. Do it again. I can't wait anymore. Make me come."

Jeremy felt Owen's hand cover his where it gripped his cock and take over, increasing the rhythm and force of the strokes. "Like that," he groaned. "Jesus, it's so good ..."

Owen was destroying Jeremy's control with his passionate response. He pushed back against his fingers, begging, "Faster. I need it. Work those magic fucking fingers in my ass and make me come."

"Greedy bastard." Jeremy sank his fingers deeper, desperately wishing his cock was the reason the man was going wild in his arms. Wishing Owen was ready to take him.

Not yet.

Jeremy's cock rocked against Owen's side as he worked him, bringing him closer and closer to the edge.

He watched his fingers disappearing inside him, heard Owen moaning with every thrust. A dark thread of satisfaction wrap around him, knowing he was the only man who'd brought Owen this much pleasure. The only man to see him like this, bent over and willing. Hungry.

"That's right," he muttered, his fingers thrusting harder. "Ride my hand. God, that's hot. This ass is begging to be fucked. Are you going to come, Owen?"

"Yes! Yes...*Fuck. God damn it,* that's—" Owen shouted his name when he came in his hand. Jeremy could feel the muscle contractions crushing his fingers with the force of the orgasm and how hard Owen was shaking. He forced himself to slow down, and then to stop, even though it was the last thing he wanted.

He pulled away and rinsed himself off before taking Owen's wilting body into his arms, his own arousal tamped down in his desire to care for him.

I've got you, baby. You came hard and so perfectly for me. I've got you.

Jeremy held the endearments in with his tongue pressed to the roof of his mouth and guided Owen out of the shower, reaching for a towel to dry him off as they walked into the bedroom.

He was too shaken for words. His reaction was too

emotional, feelings bubbling up to the surface that were difficult to contain.

What were they doing?

Ruining sex with anyone else forever. Ruining a lifetime of friendship and the life I've built around it.

That was his greatest fear. Not just because he'd seen it happen a dozen times before—a hetero guy dipping his toe in the man pool, loving it, and then running off to thump his chest and pounce on the first woman or twelve he could find to reaffirm his masculinity.

Leaving Owen safely seated on the end of the bed, Jeremy spun on his heel and went to the bathroom, using the time it took to brush his teeth to clear his head.

Owen wasn't reacting the way Jeremy would've expected at all. He was the aggressor, even when he was on the receiving end. *He* kept asking for more, as if he'd just discovered chocolate or porn. As if he couldn't get enough.

He didn't know, couldn't know how long Jeremy had dreamed of this. His own reaction was what really scared him. What could endanger their friendship. He wanted Owen. *Owen.* And now that he'd had a glimpse of what it could be like...

How hard would it be to go back?

His mind raced as he returned to the bedroom, toweling himself off while he walked. He *had* to go back. What was one night compared to nearly two decades of loyalty? Compared to the Finn family and all they'd done for him? Owen didn't have to know how deeply this was affecting him. How much more he was realizing he wanted.

Only tonight. No one would ever know.

In the bedroom, he found Owen on his feet, running his hands through his wet hair and looking around. He walked over to the dresser and opened the top drawer, pulling out a pair of suspenders. His smile was wicked.

"My turn."

CHAPTER FOUR

"What in the hell do you think you're going to do with those?" Jeremy demanded. He couldn't tear his eyes away as the bastard slid the suspenders through his other hand, stretching them.

Owen shrugged. "You don't wear ties and I didn't come prepared, so these will have to do."

"No, Owen, okay?" Jeremy held up a warning hand. "I already told you. Be happy that I shaved. That's my limit for the kinky shit."

"If you were anybody else, I might let you get away with that answer." Owen's long strides brought him within arm's reach, but in his expression, Jeremy saw something that kept him still almost against his will.

"But it wasn't anybody else I was just bent over for

and begging to finger my ass. I don't beg. But I did for you because I trust you. Are you really saying you won't even consider giving me a chance to show you something I can do for you that you might enjoy? That you won't trust me back?"

Jeremy eyed the suspenders again, silently conceding Owen's point but still wary. "What exactly is it you think I'd enjoy?"

"My undivided attention," Owen answered with a slow smile.

Jeremy shook his head. "You just came twice and you want another round?"

What about a ten-minute break so I can unscramble my brain and remember that you're only here for the night and we shouldn't be doing this?

Owen laughed. "*I* did, but you're hard as a rock. What kind of friend would I be to leave you like this? So give me a turn. Let me be in control."

Jeremy forced a glare. "Planning to hit me with those? Because you know I can kick your ass."

"I know exactly what you can do to my ass, Jeremy." Owen laughed again, softer this time. "Did Tasha scare you with her stories? I know you said she loves to shock. But this time all I want is to see you put your hands behind your back, and I'll use these to keep them there so I can do things to you that I know you'll like."

Speaking of things he liked... "No fucking without my permission."

Owen held up his hands. "I'll keep my penis to myself, I swear. I'm not going to take advantage of you. For the moment."

Jesus. Owen wanted to tie him up with his own damn suspenders? "If I agreed to do this, will you stop when I ask? Let me go if I don't like it?"

"How long have you known me? Of course I will. In the club we would have a conversation about limits and safety. We would talk until you told me every secret forbidden thing that turned you on. But this is one area where I finally know more than you do. I *know* you, Jeremy Porter. Your personality, your history—and I'm ready to learn everything there is to know about your body. I already have a pretty good idea that you'll like this. You need this. If I'm wrong, I'll stop as soon as you say the words."

Jeremy closed his eyes, shaking his head. He'd gone crazy. All the blood had permanently relocated from his brain to his cock. That was the only reason why what Owen was saying sounded appealing. He put his hands behind his back.

"One time, Owen. Just one."

"We'll see."

This wasn't his thing, he repeated to himself as Owen stepped behind him and coiled the suspenders into some kind of braided harness down his arms, tying them off at his wrists with a skill that was startling.

"Relax, Jeremy. I'm not going to hurt you. You know I'm not. Just let yourself go." Owen's voice was hypnotic, his breath warm on Jeremy's neck. "Let me take care of *you* this time."

The restraints made him feel like a raw nerve, helpless and wondering what Owen would do next. "They're a little stiff and the metal is sharp."

"Are they hurting you?"

"No."

One hot palm cupped the cheek of Jeremy's ass and he bit his lip, waiting for the sting of a slap. It didn't come. Just this. Owen's hand possessively caressing his skin, tracing the raised scar tissue of his tattoos and stroking him so tenderly Jeremy wanted to pull away.

"These are the real things," Owen mused. "I thought the Maori didn't go for tattooing visitors in the traditional way."

"My friend made an appeal from one artist to another. His cousin honored me by agreeing in exchange for a few rare comic books I brought with me."

"He honored you all over your backside and down your legs, didn't he?" Owen's touch followed the markings to his thighs. "They do it with chisels, right? Something like that had to hurt like hell."

Jeremy tipped his head back, all his attention focused on Owen's touch. "It did."

"But there's so much of it. You didn't make him stop? How did you stand the pain?"

Jeremy licked his dry lips. "There was pain, I won't lie, but most of the time I was flying on adrenaline. It's a test of endurance and will as much as anything else. And what I got in return was worth it. It was a rush."

"Pain and adrenaline," Owen repeated. "You must have a hell of a lot of endurance, Jeremy. And you liked the way it made you feel. I wish you knew how promising that sounds. How irresistible. I also wish you'd told me sooner. After *your* last birthday, for example."

"What?"

He pinched Jeremy's ass and moved until he was standing in front of him, looking down into his now open eyes. "Did I wrap you up too tight? Anything hurting? Can you still feel your fingers?"

"I'm fine," Jeremy muttered. "What about my birthday?"

Owen put his hands on Jeremy's chest and held them there. Just held them still so he could feel his own heart beating against Owen's palms. The strength in the simple touch. "As a reward for trusting me to do this, I'll tell you. Tasha's party wasn't the first time I saw you making someone's night."

Jeremy's eyes widened. "It wasn't?"

"Do you remember the concert? The woman you showed up with as your date? The one you disappeared with for some seriously acrobatic sex in the public restroom during the show you'd begged us to get tickets to?"

"Darla." He remembered her. He'd asked her to join him when he thought Tasha and Owen were both bringing dates along. He hadn't wanted to be the odd man out. But they'd both come alone and Jeremy had been kicking himself until Darla had whispered a request in his ear. Apparently stadium restrooms turned her on.

"You saw that?"

Owen's hands slid down Jeremy's torso slowly,

exploring and soothing. Arousing. "Heard it, mostly. Her. Shouting the same praise as your moaning, blond party boy. She was narrating well enough for me to get a good visual."

Shit. He didn't know what to say to that. Couldn't really think with those hands on his skin.

Owen chuckled, tracing Jeremy's hipbones, avoiding his unavoidable erection. "It—inspired me to new creative heights with my next date. And it made me wonder, the same way I did after Tasha's party. Now I know for a fact that your reputation is well-deserved." He paused, as if he were going to say more but changed his mind. "I know you said you're not a catcher—I love that term—but there's something I want you to tell me, and be honest. You have at least one butt plug around here somewhere, don't you? One you use on yourself when no one else is around?"

Jeremy's eyes widened and he felt his lips part in surprise.

"You do. See? I knew it." Owen patted his hip in approval. "You might only use it when you're alone, but you have it. Is it in a drawer by the bed? That's where I'd keep it. For those nights when I need to get off and don't have someone to impress with my Maori-esque endurance and my big fat cock. Those nights I just want to feel well and truly taken for a change."

He had to hand it to Owen. When he decided to do something, to try something new, he never did it halfway. He was a clever and seductive son of a bitch, seeming to know Jeremy's darker desires in a way no one else could. Had he learned that trick at his club? And all the touching. God, had anyone ever just touched him like this? Explored him without his being able to return the favor and distract them so they could both get what they really wanted? Jeremy was too turned on to lie. "By the bed. Second drawer."

No. Don't give in to him. Not on this. You don't let anyone do this.

But it was too late.

Owen reached behind him and gripped the knot at his wrist. "Then let's take you over to the bed."

Jeremy followed him—as if he had a choice—and watched Owen drag the pillows to the side of the bed and place one on top of the other before turning to open the first drawer.

"Hello." There was a smile in Owen's voice. "I'm guessing these are here for company? For the partners you bring home who wouldn't dare to tie you up?"

Jeremy's face was hot. "I told you it was in the second drawer."

"I know. You're not the guy that puts his own needs first, are you, Jeremy? You hide them underneath all these dirty distractions."

He closed it, thankfully, opening up the second drawer and whistling. "This is a ridged thing of beauty. Not too big but definitely not too small. I think I might need to get one for myself."

His body shuddered at Owen's words. If he wanted it, Jeremy would stretch his ass with a plug every fucking night until he was ready to take him.

Owen noticed his reaction. "You like that idea, but this isn't about *my* ass right now. It's about yours. Are you going to tell me to stop?"

"No," he whispered.

"Good boy. Assume the position."

Jeremy glared at him but let Owen lower him to the bed so that his chest was supported by, and balanced on, the pillows, his arms bound and his ass in the air. He'd never felt more naked or vulnerable.

"I can't lie, Jeremy. I'm loving this." Jeremy felt Owen's hands on his ass again, fingers digging in slightly, as if he couldn't resist. "You want more honesty? Your ass is a thing of Goddamn beauty too. With those tattoos and all that rippling muscle? It's fuckable art. And you tied up like this, ready for me to fill you with your favorite plug?" He squeezed harder, making Jeremy grit his teeth. "It's damn hot. Try to relax now. I've done this before. Not with a man, but I think I still understand the mechanics."

"I trust you." Even now, when he was questioning his own sanity and everything that had happened since he opened the door, he knew he could trust Owen with his body. "I…this isn't something I let someone do to me as a rule. But I trust you."

Owen brushed his hands lightly over Jeremy's hips, as if in praise. "Thank you."

He didn't waste any more time talking. Jeremy hissed when he felt the cold lube drizzle on his skin. Owen spread his cheeks and held them like that for long, tense minutes, making Jeremy squirm. The quickening sound of his breathing and the rhythmic flexing of his fingers on Jeremy's ass were the only clues that Owen was struggling to retain control. He muttered incoherently under his breath, and then he was pushing the plug slowly past Jeremy's resistant muscles and into his ass.

"Oh God," Jeremy groaned. It felt so different. He'd

done this to himself before but now Owen was behind him, controlling him and filling him, and it was like nothing he'd ever experienced.

Owen took his time pushing the plug all the way inside him, and then dragged it out again, inch by agonizing inch. Jeremy strained against his restraints as Owen did it again. And again. And—*sweet Jesus*—again. So slow it felt like torture. So slow it was going to make him scream. He felt close to snapping in two from the tension and need coiling inside him.

"What the hell, Owen?" he snarled. "You said you knew what you were doing."

He flinched as he heard the crack of the palm on his hip before he felt it. God, he must be truly twisted around by his desire because that sting felt good.

"I know exactly what I'm doing." Owen pressed the plug inside him again. "Do you like this, Jeremy? *I'm* hard again. Hell, I'm impressed. No little blue pill required. All I need to do is think about taking out this plug and fucking you until neither one of us can walk. I haven't been this horny since I was thirteen and read my first *Penthouse*." He pulled the plug back until only the tip was inside him. "Answer my question or I'll stop. Do you like it?"

Jeremy didn't want to answer. Didn't want to admit to it.

Another hard smack against his hip in the same spot pulled a sound of pleasure from deep inside his chest. Fuck. Why did that feel good?

Owen laughed wickedly and spanked his ass with a force and speed that knocked the breath out of Jeremy's lungs. He wouldn't cry out. He wouldn't beg for more. He couldn't stop the sounds of pleasure from escaping his lips. Couldn't stop his body from lifting to meet each blow.

"You don't like this either, do you? I've never seen someone more in need of a spanking. You know what I think, Jeremy? I think you could take more than I've ever been able to give anyone else. I think I could break my favorite paddle on your ass and you'd fucking enjoy it."

"Never gonna happen," Jeremy growled. But when Owen's palm landed hard on his ass again, he couldn't deny his body's reaction.

"Never say never." He stopped. "Let me ask you again. Do you like it? Or should I untie you and call it a day?"

"Damn it." Jeremy looked over his shoulder at Owen.

"I'd rather be fucking. I'd rather be the one doing the fucking."

Owen shook his head. "This isn't a contest, it's a question."

"Isn't it?" He gasped when Owen began to use more force with the plug, pushing it in harder. Pulling it out faster. Making it impossible to think. "*God.* You tied me up because I made you beg, now you want me to—*Oh, fuck*, Owen."

Owen pressed his cock on Jeremy's ass and rocked his hips in time with the plug. Jeremy could almost imagine Owen was fucking him. He *wanted* Owen to fuck him.

Yes. Fuck me, baby. Fuck me so hard I scream. Now while I'm bound and can't stop you. You know how bad I need it. Spank me again and make me take it.

Jeremy bit his lip so hard he tasted blood.

"Tell me you like it," Owen repeated raggedly.

"My dick is ready to stab a hole in the damn mattress. Does that answer your question? I need to come, Owen."

"At least say please."

"Fuck off."

"*Please.*"

Jeremy banged his head onto the mattress with a

shout as Owen used the plug ruthlessly. God it was good. He was so hard. He wanted to cry out. He wanted to beg. He had to beg. "*Please*, Owen. Let me come."

"That's all I wanted." Owen filled his ass with the plug until it was all the way in, making Jeremy groan. Then he crawled up onto the bed, dragging Jeremy with him toward the middle of the mattress. "On your side," he ordered sharply.

Jeremy could hardly move, the bindings making him feel totally out of control as Owen shoved him onto his side and aligned their bodies in the sixty-nine position that he loved, his cock inches away from Jeremy's mouth.

"You want to come? So do I. Suck me," Owen demanded. "I want us to come together this time."

"*Yes.*" *Oh fuck yes.* Jeremy opened his mouth and moaned when Owen spread his own thighs and thrust his hips forward, sinking his cock between Jeremy's lips. He pumped against Jeremy's face as if he couldn't help himself. Couldn't stop himself.

"Hell," Owen was groaning with every thrust. "Damn, I was right. It's even better."

Owen's mouth closed over his shaft, hungry and rough. Wild. So wild Jeremy felt his eyes rolling back in his head as lightning bolts of pleasure zapped up his spine. Owen tried to take more, but Jeremy held his hips back. Even having his own mouth fucked so hard he could barely breathe, some small coherent part of him knew Owen couldn't take the same treatment, no matter how good it would feel.

You taste so good. Suck me harder, Owen. Need to come with you.

Owen's thigh went taut against Jeremy's cheek and he knew. He could taste it on his tongue. Owen was one thrust away from coming. Jeremy felt the plug in his ass and Owen's mouth on him and he couldn't wait anymore either. He swirled his tongue and swallowed Owen's cock where it pressed against the back of his throat, and then they were both coming, both moaning and shaking against each other as they found release.

Jeremy was drowning. Flying. He'd been so thoroughly taken he didn't know which end was up. His limbs were shaking while he hungrily licked Owen's shaft, unable to stop until Owen rolled him onto his stomach and undid his restraints.

"That's the look I love," Owen murmured gently. "Now who's a natural? I had a feeling you would be."

Jeremy felt hands and lips on his arms, and he

couldn't stop himself from turning back toward Owen and pulling him down for a kiss that said everything he couldn't.

He didn't want it to end, but it had to. This was all they could have.

Owen, what are you doing to me? What are we doing?

CHAPTER FIVE

"Another beer, Jeremy?"

He looked up at Owen's sister and nodded with an absent smile. "Thanks, Jen. I'd love one."

"Anything for you, dimples," she said with a wink, her light blue eyes reminding him of Owen's. "You look great without the beard by the way. Ten years younger. Don't get me wrong, you had the whole dangerous artistic biker thing going on, and it was hot, but you really do have a handsome face. It reminds me what a crush I had on you when I was just an innocent tween. Too bad I'm getting married, because I could get into a lot of trouble with a bad boy like you."

"Don't patronize me, little Finn. The bad boy is now a dirty old man."

Jennifer Finn rolled her eyes. "Tell someone who doesn't know. Still, it could work. My brothers like you better than they like their future in-law."

Jeremy barely held back a snort. They'd like a fungus better than they liked Jennifer's fiancé, Scott, but he wasn't going to be the one to say it. Every time anyone did, Jen just dug in and reminded them of Scott's horrible childhood. She'd started rooting for the underdog in middle school and she still wasn't ready to throw in the towel. She was going to soft-heart her way into an unhappy marriage if the Finns didn't shake some sense into her soon.

He grinned at her. "The Finn boys don't like me—I'm prettier than they are and they know it."

Jen laughed. "I know it too. So does that hot guy at the end of the bar who keeps asking me questions about you."

"Don't start. You know my rule—no pick-ups at your family's place. I wouldn't want to give anyone a heart attack."

"Spoilsport," Jennifer pouted. "No one else is around tonight. Anyway, Dad wouldn't blame you, and even if he did, Seamus will be taking over soon and he's got plans to bring in a younger crowd with healthier, less narrow-minded hearts. Come on, look at that guy. He's a Latin hunk of sexy and he's totally into you. I suppose if you want to let him down easy I could let you flirt with me. Though if he's anything like you, it might make him more interested."

"Little Finn, you are trouble," he said, shaking his head, "and you're sounding like Natasha. What has she been filling your head with? We shouldn't have let you make her a bridesmaid. You two are obviously spending way too much time together."

"And we still have five months to go." Jen looked around and then lowered her voice. "Speaking of Tasha, she's taking me to her club for a special bachelorette party soon. One of her friends is going to…well, we're negotiating. That's what they call it, Jeremy. *Negotiating.* You basically have to sign a contract to get kinky. Isn't that wild?"

Oh, hell no. "Does Owen know about this?"

"No, he doesn't, and don't you dare tell him, Jeremy Porter." She fiddled with her strawberry blonde braid the way she always did when she was nervous or excited. "I'm twenty-four not twelve. I can do whatever I want. But if he happens to show up and give me grief? I'll threaten to tell our feminist mother how *he* spends all his free time lately. That would be enough to scare anyone into silence."

Just lately he spent it with me, he thought, lowering his head into his hand and sighing. He wondered how Ellen Finn would respond to *that* information.

Somehow he didn't think they'd be any more pleased than they would be about Jen getting her kink on at Tasha's club. Though his transgression would merit far worse than a lecture.

"I wish I didn't know this," he mumbled into his palm. "Why do I know this?"

Jen took his hand off his face and squeezed it. "Because I know you'll understand and keep my secrets. You always have."

He squeezed back. "And I always will, little Finn. Still, this is a bit more intense than the average bachelorette shindig. Why don't you get a stripper and objectify him with your friends like a normal girl?"

"I just want to try it once. I'm going to marry Scott, and I know him well enough to realize he won't be the kind of husband that wants to experiment with that sort of thing. If you want to know the truth, he likes to—"

"I don't," Jeremy interrupted rapidly. "I really don't want to know the truth. At all."

She giggled and he studied her through narrowed eyes. "All three of your brothers would take turns kicking my ass if they found out I knew about this and didn't talk you out of it. They won't hear it from me, but I have to tell you, I'm not liking the idea of you negotiating with one of Tasha's friends."

"You're one of her friends." She grinned. "Let's negotiate. If you want to let that man pick you up while I watch, maybe even kiss him, I might get enough of a vicarious thrill to change my mind and cancel my date at the club."

Jeremy shook his head and took a drink. "Tempting as that is, your brother's going to be here any minute. How about I promise not to say a word if you stop trying to hook me up before he gets here?"

"Have it your way." Someone called her name and she moved to the other end of the bar, leaving Jeremy staring into his glass mug.

That conversation had been disconcerting as hell. He needed to have a talk with Tasha. Was she trying to drive Owen crazy by leading his sister over to the dark side, or was it something else? Was she using a different method of persuasion to show Jennifer that she had more options than Scott? If so, it was already more successful than the Finn frontal assault her brothers Stephen and Seamus had attempted.

At least it had temporarily taken his mind off the reason he was here. The reason he couldn't make himself get up and leave, even though that was exactly what he wanted to do.

Owen had ordered him to come.

Jeremy hadn't seen him in the two days since his birthday. The last time, he'd been lying in bed, watching Owen dress so he could go home and change before work. He'd kept his hands laced under his pillow, his short nails digging painfully into his skin so he wouldn't reach for him and try to convince him to stay.

When Owen sat down on the bed and kissed him, it hadn't felt like a goodbye, and he'd let himself fantasize that it wasn't. But his absence and the light of day had brought Jeremy's doubts and fears to the surface, and reaffirmed his decision. There were so many reasons there couldn't be a repeat performance. Good reasons why he couldn't let things get sexual again. Their friendship, his close ties with the Finn family...

Those damn suspenders.

He'd never allowed himself to be restrained before. He'd told Owen he didn't judge, but he couldn't help wondering what it was that people enjoyed about being on the receiving end of that type of relationship. Being powerless.

Jeremy was always in control. He'd had to be. He'd never had the family life Owen enjoyed. His parents had always been too caught up in their own brawling to express anything but disappointment in their introvert son, who'd spent all his time drawing at the park or buried in a comic book. They'd finally found something they agreed on enough to stop fighting when they caught him in the bathroom with a magazine of male nudes. *No son of ours...* Insert cliché here.

At fourteen, he'd found himself kicked out of his own house—not that he'd ever felt like he belonged there. The heroes in his favorite stories were usually switched at birth or alien babies from another planet, and he'd spent a lot of time imagining he was too. In fact, the scenarios he dreamed up for his *real* family were the basis for those first amateurish comics he'd drawn after he moved in with his aunt, a woman who preferred cuddling a bottle to raising a fourteen-year-old boy with sexuality issues.

His dad had shoved him out the door with just enough money to pay part of her rent for a month, and she'd let him stay as long as he worked a part-time job after school and paid enough rent to keep her in wine boxes and forties. But her grungy little studio had never been his home any more than his parents' house had, which was just one more reason why he'd spent as much time as he could at the Finns'.

That was his life, and Jeremy had dealt with it. He'd worked hard, and with Mr. Finn's help, he'd won a scholarship for college, majoring in art. Then he'd created the popular series of comic books about a demon on his own in the big city, trying to make amends for his past, and it had taken off right before graduation. Now he owned his own house, had money in savings and didn't owe anyone a damn thing. Didn't depend on anyone for his security and well-being.

Except the Finns. He owed them. He depended on them and didn't know what he'd do without them.

He shook off his guilt and took another drink. For the most part he was independent and in control. And it was the same with sex. He chose his partners and he was always the one to walk away. Tasha was his only exception, but even she respected his tastes when it came to men. He wasn't one of those submissive males who liked to have his will taken away. He didn't change himself—shave his fucking beard—just to please his lover.

Until now.

Owen got to him. Made him want to give in to him in a way he never had with anyone before. Jeremy didn't like it. Didn't like how close he'd been to begging for that paddle. For Owen's dick.

And he hated how uncertain he felt the next day. That was new too. The neediness. The self-doubt. It was just sex. He didn't need comforting after sex, damn it.

So he'd taken the necessary steps. He'd changed the outgoing message on his phone, saying he was drawing on deadline and he'd call back when he could. A few days, maybe a week should be enough, he'd thought. Long enough that it wasn't so fresh in their minds, and they could put it aside and move on. Tasha's messages were concerned. Owen's were frustratingly short and enigmatic. He hadn't answered either of them, and he'd made sure he was out running errands or grabbing dinner whenever Owen could be driving home from his construction site.

He'd tried to get some work done so he wouldn't be a liar as well as a coward, but he hadn't been able to draw a straight line. He also hadn't come up with any epiphanies or reasonable explanations for what they'd experienced together. If anything, spending the last two days alone had made him feel more vulnerable. More out of control. Owen was all he could think about. Every hour was spent reliving their one night. The things Owen had said. The things he'd done.

When he'd gotten that text a few hours ago telling him to meet here or face the consequences, Jeremy was at the end of his rope. Ignoring Owen wasn't working, and that message was clear—he wasn't going to take no for an answer this time.

Maybe he just wanted to assure himself they were still friends, though Owen had never been insecure. Maybe he wouldn't talk about it at all. It would be better if he didn't, Jeremy told himself. He could show Owen he was fine, that they could still hang out like they used to and that their friendship hadn't been irrevocably damaged. That had to be what Owen wanted. For all their sakes.

And then he would go home and find a way to forget how it felt to be with him. How right.

He'd just taken another drink when the man from the end of the bar appeared beside him, leaning his elbow casually on the counter. "I know you saw me and I can feel the 'stay away' vibes you're throwing down, but you look like you could use someone to talk to and you're too attractive to be sitting alone. Can I buy you another beer?"

He studied the stranger. "Does that line usually work for you?"

The man laughed. "Would I sound arrogant if I said yes?"

Jen was right. He was hot. Young and handsome, with dark eyes that sparkled with interest and an honest, open approach that appealed to Jeremy. He knew instinctively that he could get this man home and out of his clothes in under an hour. Hell, maybe he should. Maybe a one-night stand with someone who knew what they were asking for and could take what Jeremy needed to give was just what the doctor ordered to get his mind off Owen.

He waited for the hum of arousal and excitement that usually came with a potential new conquest, but there was nothing. Jeremy sighed, knowing it wasn't going to happen. Not tonight. Not for a while. "I appreciate it, but I'm afraid I'll have to pass."

"Are you sure?" The stranger lowered his voice and leaned closer. "I *am* arrogant, but from the look of you I think you'd know exactly how to put me in my place."

Jeremy chuckled and started to refuse again, but before he had a chance, Owen arrived beside them and beat him to the punch.

"He passed. Weren't you paying attention?"

The man's eyes widened slightly and he turned around to see Owen towering over him, his blond hair mussed from the wind, his blue eyes icy and threatening. "You should leave now."

"I didn't know this seat was taken," the man mumbled, throwing money on the bar and walking out of the pub without another word. Jeremy watched Owen glare at his back until he disappeared, more than a little surprised at his reaction.

"Bad day?"

Owen turned back to him and Jeremy actually felt a knot of anxiety forming in his stomach. He did *not* look happy.

"We need to talk."

"Hey, big brother." Jen walked over and leaned forward on the bar in front of them. "You look like hell. You didn't fire Scott, did you? It was my idea to get you that stripper, in case you were mad."

"I could have gone all year without knowing that."

Owen rubbed the back of his neck with his palm and nodded. "But it has been a tough day. In fact, that's why I asked Jeremy to drop by. A friend of ours is making some bad decisions and I need his help getting it sorted out. Beers and darts later?"

Jen frowned in concern but nodded. "You're on."

Owen gripped Jeremy's arm. "Let me fill you in out back."

Shit. He thought they'd come here so they wouldn't be alone, but it was clear Owen had something to say that he didn't want anyone else to hear. Was he going to tell him to stay away from his family? From him? Was he going to say he was drunk that night and he didn't remember how it started or why? "Sure."

They walked past the dartboards and the bathrooms, into the small kitchen that was only open for lunch and out the back door. The back alley of Finn's was narrow, without a lot of places for privacy. Owen kept walking until he'd moved past the large trash bin and into the shadows.

Jeremy followed at a slower pace. Owen was definitely upset. "What's up?"

Owen took him by surprise when he grabbed him by his shirt and flung him against the brick wall a little harder than necessary. The air left his lungs in a whoosh.

"*What's up?*" Owen sounded incredulous. "Are you seriously asking that?"

Jeremy frowned, holding up his hands. "Owen, calm down. You said you wanted to talk."

"Oh, I've wanted to talk for two days, Jeremy. You haven't answered my calls. Then I came over after work yesterday and you weren't there. Where the hell were you?"

Jeremy swallowed hard. "Dinner. I must have been picking up dinner. And I was going to answer your messages. I was busy."

"Do you think I'm an idiot? That I haven't known you for two decades? Seen you in action? You were avoiding me like I was one of your one-night stands. One of your little third boys. *Me*."

"I was giving you space," Jeremy shot back. Owen had avoided him for three weeks, and *he* hadn't gone off like this. "And it was a one-night stand, wasn't it? We agreed it was only going to be one night. What the hell, man?"

"I didn't agree to you acting like I didn't exist. I wanted to make sure you were okay, and you didn't let me because you were too busy running from what we did." Owen stepped closer and reached out to grip his wrist, guiding his hand toward his cock. "You were avoiding *this*. Giving me space I didn't ask for and pissing me off. Then I walk into the bar and you're already working on lining up someone else for the night."

Jeremy pushed Owen away roughly, trying to ignore the fact that his knuckles had brushed against one hell of an erection. "He wanted to buy me a drink, that's all. Jesus, Owen, stop it. Someone could walk by."

"Do you think I care?" He gasped as he found himself pinned between Owen's body and the wall. "I don't give a damn. You're not going anywhere until we deal with this. And he didn't want a drink. He wanted to fuck you and you were thinking about it."

"This is your *family's* place. Let's at least talk about this somewhere else."

"We're talking about it now. Was it because I tied you up? Did liking it scare you?"

"We can't. This isn't the time or... Owen. It's not a good idea."

Owen responded by kissing him, tangling their tongues in a way that had Jeremy melting back against the wall. He'd known he loved it, but he hadn't realized how much he'd missed it, needed it until now. His lips. His kiss.

"Did it scare you?"

"No," Jeremy gasped. "Yes… Damn it, I can't think when you're kissing me."

"Don't think. Just feel," Owen said between biting kisses. "If you won't talk to me, won't let down your guard any other way, I'll take what I can get. You can't leave me like this for days, Jeremy. Tell me I'm not alone in feeling this way. Say you want me again."

"You know I do, damn it."

"I know it," Owen agreed. "You seem to be the one trying to forget."

Jeremy's heart was pounding and his cock was painfully hard. Seeing Owen like this, so hungry and aggressive, was robbing him of his will to resist.

Owen unzipped his own pants impatiently, dragging Jeremy's hand back against his stomach and groaning when his fingers couldn't resist sliding down and curling around that hot, bare flesh. "*There*. God *yes*. You did this to me. I've never been like this before. I can't think, I can't work; I can't do anything but remember your mouth on me. You shouldn't have been so good, Jeremy, because now I need it. I *need you*."

"Owen—"

"Get on your knees for me. Let me feel it again." His voice was low and harsh. Commanding.

"Jesus," Jeremy whispered, unable to stop himself from falling to his knees on the dirty concrete. Here in the fucking alley?

Anywhere he wanted.

CHAPTER SIX

Owen's groan was guttural when Jeremy opened his mouth over his erection. "*Yes*." He gripped Jeremy's head between his hands and rocked forward with shallow thrusts. "Christ, you're a sexy bastard. I'm still mad at you but I can't resist this. I'm out of control and I'm not sure I like it. It's never happened before. Not like this. Jesus, you're sucking me so good, I know you love it. *Ah*…yeah, damn it, just like that."

Jeremy moaned. He did love it. Loved Owen's taste, loved how tightly he gripped his head, setting the pace and making Jeremy take every thick inch. And the things he was saying made him so hard he ached. It made him want to come more than he wanted to breathe. He wanted to make Owen come and know he'd driven him that wild. To know he wasn't alone in this obsession.

Owen took one of his hands off Jeremy's head and pressed it against the wall for balance as his hips started to pump faster, deeper into Jeremy's mouth.

"God, that's hot," he muttered. "This is what that asshole wanted. I could see the way he was looking at you. If he knew how talented your tongue is, how big your cock is, I might have had to fight him for you." He inhaled shakily when Jeremy reached up to cup his tight sac. "I would have. I swear I was ready to drag him outside in front of everyone, because this is mine. I want it more than he does. I want it all the time."

Oh God. Jeremy moaned, sucking harder.

"You like hearing that? Then I'll tell you more. I want to wake up with this mouth on me. Keep you tied up and under my damn desk at work so I can have you sucking me off all fucking day."

Jeremy was trembling at the images Owen created, one hand pressed hard against his own erection as he relaxed his throat and took Owen deeper.

"And then at night," Owen rasped, his breath coming in rapid pants as he sped closer to his climax. "At night, if you're good, I'll let you take me. Throw me down and fuck me the way I know you want to. I've been thinking about that too. Do you want to know what's filling my ass right now? What I bought two days ago so I could get ready for you? *Oh, Jesus, Jeremy.* Don't stop." His thrusts were fast now, desperate. *"It's so good. Fuck."*

Jeremy's own shout was muffled around Owen's hot flesh as he came in his pants like a teenager with his first hard-on when the salty release filled his mouth.

Want you, baby. Need to get inside. Need you.

After a few minutes where they were both recovering, Jeremy leaned back and looked down, swearing when he saw the wet spot on his jeans. Owen helped him stand, looking flushed and sexy and absolutely shameless about what they'd just done.

"Jeremy." Owen squeezed his hand, rubbed his arms gently. "That was amazing."

Jeremy was still recovering. Owen had liked seeing him on his knees in the alley. Jesus, right here in the alley.

"I can't go back into the pub like this, damn it. Your sister—" He gestured toward his pants.

"I'll handle that," Owen assured him calmly, adjusting himself and zipping up his jeans before running his hands through his hair. "You're going to go to the parking lot, get in your car and drive straight home to wait for me. I'll be right behind you."

"Bossy son of a bitch," Jeremy muttered, thrown by the intensity of his reaction, and how quickly he'd given in despite his decision not to. "Who invited you?"

"We still need to talk." Owen leaned into him and kissed his neck, scraping his teeth along the tight cords of muscle. "You don't like that you like it, I know," he whispered. "But we'll both like what you get for doing what I say. I promise."

He walked away and Jeremy shoved his hands in his pockets, cursing himself for his weakness. He couldn't stop this train, even though he knew it was destined to go off the rails. Jeremy didn't have much control when it came to Owen. All the man had to do was look at him the right way or say a word and he laid it all at his damn feet. Ending this would be the smart thing. The safe thing. But Owen would have to be the one to do it, and right now, it looked like that was the last thing he wanted.

Jeremy drove back to his house, thinking about what Owen had said. While he'd been trying to back off and give him an out, his stubborn lover had gotten a plug to stretch his ass for Jeremy's cock.

He had it in right now.

His best friend wanted to be his lover. Wanted him.

He pulled his truck into the driveway and shut off the ignition, sitting in the dark and letting it sink in. Owen wanted Jeremy to fuck him. One erotic fantasy after another played out in his head. Lifting Owen against the wall, his legs over Jeremy's arms as he lowered him onto his cock. Taking Owen on the floor, in the shower, the sound of his cries as he came.

Jeremy unbuttoned his jeans and lowered the zipper, pulling out the dick that was already growing hard again as he let his dreams play out. Owen said *he* was obsessed? He couldn't possibly have it as bad as Jeremy.

"Owen," he murmured, stroking himself. "You're tight, baby. Gonna fuck your ass so hard."

But he knew when he was done Owen wouldn't be able to leave well enough alone. He'd have to have his turn. Jeremy groaned, knowing that he would resist, and that he would eventually give in—because he wanted it more than he'd ever thought possible. With Owen. Only with Owen.

A conversation from the other night had him imagining Owen on top. Being pinned down as Owen demanded his submission, whispering filthy things in his ear as he took what he wanted.

"This is mine. Tell me, Jeremy. Tell me this ass belongs to me. Beg me to fuck it. Beg me to stuff this greedy hole with my cock."

"Yours," Jeremy mumbled, pressing his head back against the seat as his hand worked his shaft. "Please. Only you."

The knock on his window made him jump like a kid with his hand caught in the cookie jar. Or a teenage boy caught with his hand down his pants.

Owen was watching him.

Jeremy rolled down the window, his cheeks burning. "You got here fast."

Owen lifted one eyebrow. "I know I didn't tell you to go *inside* the house to wait for me, but I thought that was a given."

Jesus, was that what he was doing? *Obeying* Owen like some mindless slave? "Fuck you, man."

Already rattled, Jeremy got out and slammed the truck door behind him, his long strides taking him to his front door and inside before some random neighbor looked out and noticed his state of undress. He was seriously messed up.

"Fucking is the plan." Owen followed him into the living room carrying a stuffed gym bag. When he saw

Jeremy's eyes fixed on it, he laughed. "I came prepared this time. Some clothes and a few supplies you might enjoy."

Jeremy ground his teeth. The bastard took a hell of a lot for granted. "I thought *talking* was the plan. You had an overnight bag in your car before you came to meet me?"

Owen nodded, determination etched into his handsome face. "We can do both. And the plan was not leaving without you, Jeremy. You know how stubborn I can be."

His strange calm should have aggravated Jeremy's temper. Instead, he found himself following his lead, taking a breath and collecting his scattered wits. "I do. I'm just not sure why you're being stubborn about *this*." He nodded at the bag. "Is this your subtle way of saying you want to stay for the weekend?"

"It's my not-so-subtle way of saying I'm staying the night. Let's leave it at that for now." When Jeremy frowned, Owen sighed. "I get why you backed off, Jeremy, I do. Why you decided to limit us to that night. I don't like that you didn't talk to me, but I get it. Neither one of us was expecting this to happen. But now that it has, you can't deny how good it feels. And I refuse to apologize for wanting more of you."

Jeremy ran a hand over his face, still startled to feel a smooth jaw line instead of facial hair. He had to ask, "How much more? Because I've got to tell you, Owen, I'm not sure I'm willing to put our friendship on the line for sex, no matter how great it is. And I can't get my head around why *you* seem to be willing to risk it."

"How long have you been having sex with Natasha, Jeremy?"

Jeremy's eyes narrowed. "A while."

"Please," Owen laughed, his smile tight. "The first time you two fooled around we were juniors in high school. And you've been on her fuck buddy speed dial for years now. She comes and goes and it hasn't hurt your friendship at all. In a way, I think it's made you closer. What's so different about this?"

Everything, and they both knew it. This wasn't the same. This was insanity. Lust on a scale he'd rarely experienced, if ever. And of all the men his body could have decided to go crazy over, it had to be Owen Finn. "Where should I begin? How about with the whole you're-not-gay issue?"

Owen dropped the bag at his feet and moved closer. "I know where *you* want to begin, but I'm not willing to let you label this. I know who and what I am, and I'm here because I want to be. Period. Are you going to look me in the eye and tell me you don't want this as badly as I do? That you'd really be okay if I told you to forget it before we got it out of our systems? Would you really be satisfied with that?"

He reached for Jeremy's shirt and started undoing the buttons. "Just because this is new for me doesn't mean I can't tell how intense the chemistry is. It's not just me. Fifteen minutes ago you were on your knees sucking my cock. Five minutes ago you were jerking off in your truck, knowing I was coming to give you more. Don't hide behind excuses when we both know you'd do anything to fuck me. Admit it to yourself at least. Admit you want this."

Knowing he already had, Jeremy sighed in defeat. Jesus, Owen really was one stubborn son of a bitch. But if he was that determined to give Jeremy exactly what he wanted, why would he be stupid enough to resist?

He grabbed the collar of Owen's flannel and yanked, the snaps wrenching open easily beneath his hands.

"You win." Dragging Owen's shirt off, he tossed it on the floor. "I admit it. I want you. More now than I ever have, and I've wanted you for longer than you'd be comfortable knowing."

Blue eyes lit with interest. "Screw comfortable and tell me. How long?"

"Let me put it this way—I had half your team in college trying to work this ache out of my system."

Owen paused in the act of stripping off Jeremy's shirt. "Bullshit."

"Tasha helped." Jeremy smiled wickedly, enjoying the surprise and arousal in Owen's expression. "And it was only a few defensive linemen. But you'd be surprised how willing they were to risk exposure so I could live out my fantasy of sharing the team shower with you after a game."

"Which ones?"

He shook his head. "You'll die wondering. I don't kiss and tell."

Owen licked his lips. "You never said anything."

"And you never woke up without a girl in your bed."

Owen unzipped his pants and stepped out of them thoughtfully. "I have this sudden desire to visit our old alma mater and chain you to that shower for a week. I'm thinking of a million ways I could torture you for telling me that story."

Jeremy chuckled. "You wanted an admission."

"That wasn't what I had in mind. You might not know this, but I can be a possessive man."

"Of your things," Jeremy acknowledged. "Not people." Owen was protective of family and friends, but never possessive.

"You'd be surprised. I am. I won't tell you what I wanted to do with that jerk at the bar who was sizing you up for a ride, or what I thought about last night while I was sitting in your driveway."

"I told you I went out for dinner."

He shrugged, his muscled body tense. "And I told you I knew you were lying. I was wondering if you were with that screamer Tasha introduced you to at the party. If you were giving him more of what I wanted. It took all of my willpower not to call her and get his name and address."

Jeremy was removing his boots but he looked up at that. "I don't even remember his name. It was just a one-time thing."

"With all those notches on your bedpost, I'm not surprised you can't keep track."

"I'm not *that* bad. I hear you've got me beat, Master Finn."

They were naked, their clothes in a pile at their feet,

and Jeremy hissed when Owen reached out to trace his bare hip. "Tasha again? Someone needs to take a flogger to that woman's ass. Not that I'm denying it. I like sex. And this year has not been one for restraint. Maybe it's because thirty-five was looming and my baby sister got engaged. But you're right there with me, buddy. You are as sexual an animal as any I've seen. Maybe we're getting that mid-life crisis issue over with early."

"Is that what this is?" Jeremy hated that he sounded vulnerable, so he focused on keeping his expression neutral. When Owen slid his hands around his waist and leaned in to lick his nipple, the façade crumbled and Jeremy groaned.

"I don't know," Owen admitted softly. "But whatever it is, I know I can't let it stop. I won't, not yet. So while we're finding out, I want you to do something for me."

God, yes. Anything. Just do that again. "What?"

Owen looked up from Jeremy's chest to meet his gaze. "As long as we're doing this, satisfying our curiosity...I'm the only man who gets to touch you."

As if he could think about anyone else when Owen was with him like this. Touching him. Seducing him with his lips and hands. "What about you?"

"No man but you."

Jeremy noticed the amusement in Owen's eye just in time to bite back his instinctive *fuck that*. "Glad to know *women* aren't off limits for either of us," he countered without missing a beat.

Owen was no longer amused. "Just us, Jeremy."

He bit his cheek so he wouldn't smile. *Sucker.* "Agreed."

"And you'll give me a blowjob whenever I want," Owen added, daring Jeremy to argue.

Jeremy sighed, knowing it was going to happen regardless. Now who was the sucker? "Fine."

"Good. We've talked enough, don't you think? We have our agreement. I've been wanting this for days, and I don't think I can wait another minute."

He cupped Owen's face in his hands, giving in.

"Neither can I."

Jeremy wasn't sure how much time had passed. How long they'd been rolling around on the bed, a tangle of arms and legs sliding against each other, shining with sweat and need.

Not long enough.

He couldn't stop kissing Owen. No matter how hard

he was or how much he ached for release, he wanted to take his time. Owen's lips, the scent of his skin as Jeremy kissed a path across his smooth chest and traced every lean muscle of his torso with his tongue… He didn't want to rush a single second of it.

This was the body he'd lusted after. The one he'd dreamed of and compared every man he'd ever been with to. It deserved his attention. Deserved to be savored. A seduction instead of the violent fucking Jeremy wanted to give him.

His first time…

He scraped his teeth along Owen's hip and smiled at the jump of his cock and his agonized groan.

"This is torture." Owen gasped when Jeremy sucked on the skin of his inner thigh. "God, your mouth. I'm ready to beg for it again, but you know what I want. I won't let you distract me."

"And I won't let *you* distract *me*. I'm enjoying myself."

Owen reached down to tangle his fingers in Jeremy's hair. "I don't need foreplay. I've been ready for more since I left this bed the last time."

Jeremy pressed his erection into the bed and ground his teeth together. "You're not ready. You think because you can take a plug you're ready?"

Owen rolled away from Jeremy and got on his knees, his expression challenging. "Never been anybody's first time before? We know that's not true, unless those defensive linemen were more experienced than you're letting on. Lucky for you, I'm the king of first times."

His smile was a dare. "There's a trick to it. Are you paying attention? You stick your big fucking cock in and make me like it." He shrugged. "If you don't think you can do that, I'm more than happy to give you pointers. Or maybe I should show you by example."

Jeremy growled and pushed himself off the bed, his hands on his hips. He couldn't tell if Owen wanted to fuck or fight, or both. "You're pushing, Owen. Why do you keep pushing?"

"Because you won't." He shrugged, his gaze dropping to stare at Jeremy's erection. "Because it's me and for some reason that makes you nervous. If I have to top you from the bottom, I will. I'm not a total innocent, Jeremy. I know the mechanics. I know what's going to happen. I'm asking for it. Demanding it. I don't need to be seduced into compliance."

"No, what you need is something shut you up," Jeremy rasped. "But more than that, you need to be damn sure what you're asking for, because—" His voice cracked, just enough for him to hate the weakness. "I don't think I could take it if you wanted me to stop."

Without a word Owen followed him off the bed, reaching for one of the condoms on the bedside table. He tore open the foil and started rolling the latex down Jeremy's shaft.

"Jesus, Owen," he gasped at the skilled touch.

"This *is* going to happen, Jeremy." When he was done he turned his back, bending over and placing his forearms on this bed.

He pressed his forehead into his fists and then looked up over his shoulder at Jeremy. "I'm used to being on top and calling the shots. I've never wanted something so much I was willing to give that up. But I'm here. I want this and I won't change my mind."

Jeremy moved closer and laid his palm on Owen's back, needing to touch him. He could hear it in his voice—the same vulnerability he felt. Owen Finn wasn't used to giving up control, but now he was demanding Jeremy take it from him.

"Tell me you want me." Jeremy's voice was ragged and laced with need as he lowered his hands to the cheeks of Owen's ass, his attention on the plug between them.

"What in the hell do you think I've been saying?" Owen inhaled sharply when Jeremy tugged on the plug and drew it slowly out. "God that's—I want it, Jeremy, okay? I want you inside me. So much it hurts more than anything you think you're going to do to me."

Jeremy bit his lip as he replaced the plug with his lube-covered finger, pushing inside Owen's ass. It was still tight but the muscles yielded more readily to his touch. "Tell me how the plug felt. The first time you put it in."

Owen was rocking against Jeremy's hand and it was the sexiest thing he'd ever seen. "I couldn't breathe, I felt so full. There was pain but it was the best kind. Everything at once, you know?"

"I know," Jeremy answered softly, adding another finger.

"I was thinking about you. Thinking about taking all of you when I put it in." He tilted his hips, asking for more. "Oh, that's good... All I had to do was think about you fucking me and I loved it. If you liked what I did to you half as much as I loved that, I don't know why you made me stay away."

He couldn't do it again. Couldn't refuse this man

who was offering him everything. Jeremy pulled his fingers out and guided his shaft to that tight ring of muscles, gripping Owen's hip with his free hand. "I want you to breathe out, Owen. Breathe out and relax."

"Jesus," Owen whispered so softly he almost missed it. He blew out a big breath and Jeremy pressed forward, feeling the resistance before the head of his cock pushed inside. "*Jeremy.*"

"Fuck," Jeremy growled, his fingers digging into Owen's skin as he pressed forward and felt tight muscles resisting, squeezing him before giving way.

More, baby. So tight. I need more. Need to get it all inside you.

"Oh *mother fucking*—!" Owen's hands were clawing and dragging the covers closer to him, desperate for something to hold onto. Jeremy could hear his labored breathing, see the muscles rippling in his back as he struggled to hold himself still. "God. *Oh God.*"

"Do you want to stop?"

Owen groaned loud and long when Jeremy followed the question with another thrust, loving the way Owen's ass gripped his cock like a hungry fist.

Don't make me stop, baby. Can't stop. Need to take you.

"So tight," he snarled. "Is it too much, damn it? Should I stop?"

"Don't stop. Fuck. *Fuck*, don't. I want it. God help me, I *need* it."

Jeremy needed it too. He needed to get all the way inside. One of his hands curved around Owen's shoulder, gripping the strong muscles there as Jeremy tilted his hips forward with more force, making them both shout when he was finally as far as he could go.

"Is this what you needed?" he moaned. "What you've been asking for?"

Owen nodded jerkily, his groans incoherent as he adjusted to the new sensations. "Jesus, I can't believe I can take you. I said I could but you're so big I wasn't sure. God, you're filling me up, Jeremy."

"Stop talking," Jeremy ordered, his jaw clenched. He was trying to keep himself still, trying to hold back. "I won't be able to give you the time you need if you keep talking."

Owen's laugh was breathless and broken. "It gets you hot, hearing me talk about your cock, doesn't it? I can't help it, Jeremy. God, your big fucking cock could turn a straight man gay. Let me prove it to you. Call me Exhibit A and fuck me."

"I told you to *stop talking*." But it was too late. Jeremy had enough restraint to make sure he didn't hurt him, and that was all. He had to move.

His strokes were slow and shallow at first, but the sounds Owen was making, the way he felt around him, shredded his good intentions. Jeremy pressed his chest against Owen's back, the hand on his hip sliding around until it was gripping his thick erection.

"Yes." Owen shuddered against him. "I love your hands on me."

"You're so hard for me," Jeremy whispered hotly in response. "I want you to come screaming my name with me buried in your ass. But not yet. I don't want to stop yet. Can you take more?"

"Yes," Owen moaned. "Jesus, *yes*. More."

Jeremy bared his teeth as he pulled back his hips and then thrust deeper, trying to pace himself so he didn't go too fast. Wasn't too rough.

Hold back, he whispered to himself. *Keep control. His first time. Don't want it to end.*

But once again, Owen was proving to be a quick study. His hand covered Jeremy's over his erection, setting a faster rhythm, letting Jeremy know what he wanted.

"Yeah," he groaned. "You're in me so deep."

Deep. I'm fucking you so deep, baby. I'm finally inside you and fucking you and you love it. You fucking love it and I don't ever want to stop.

"Owen…" Jeremy's moan was raw and aching. "You're making it hard to hold back. I've wanted it for so long. Fuck, it's good. Want to fuck you so hard."

"Do it," Owen bit out, his hand tightening over Jeremy's on his erection.

"No. No, I have to—"

"I'm close, Jeremy. I want to come while you hold me down and pound my ass with that big fat fucking cock. I need you to do that for *me* this time. Need you."

A red fog of lust and need surrounded him and he knew he was losing the battle. He placed his hand on Owen's head, pressing his cheek into the mattress. "Come then. Come for me and I'll give you what you need."

Owen shouted as he found his release, his muscles clenching forcefully in reaction around Jeremy's cock, as if he'd been waiting for permission. Then all Jeremy felt was the ass he was claiming. Owning. He pumped into it harder than he should have, faster than he meant to, growling at the tight fit.

God, I love it. Love your ass. Love…

Jeremy watched Owen's mouth open on a silent shout as he took the restrained version of the rough pounding he'd demanded. Hopefully that was pleasure on his face, because Jeremy couldn't stop. Wouldn't stop. He was too close. "*Owen.*"

His orgasm hit him like a twenty-foot wave crashing over his body. He couldn't breathe. Couldn't see. Couldn't do anything but cry out and let it wash him away.

Owen was beneath him. His Owen.

Mine.

Jeremy shuddered and he leaned against Owen, trembling as he fought to recover his senses. God, he smelled good. Felt good.

Best I've ever had. So good. Need to kiss you.

Owen blew out a huff of a laugh as Jeremy nuzzled his neck. "You already need to shave again, you beast."

"Bossy," Jeremy murmured, lifting himself off of Owen and slowly pulling out with a shaky breath. "Let's get you into the shower first."

Owen groaned as he pushed off the bed and got to his feet. "Shit, I can't feel my legs."

"Want me to carry you?"

"Fuck off," Owen laughed, turning to look up at him with something in his expression that made Jeremy's heart pound a little harder. "Give me a second to catch my breath and I'll be ready for more."

Hell. "Shower first."

He forced himself to move away from Owen and staggered into the bathroom, turning on the water. His mind was in turmoil, racing from one question to the next. Had that really happened? Had everything in his world just changed forever? Was Owen okay? Was he going to demand a turn now?

"Jeremy?"

He looked over his shoulder and found Owen smiling softly, a bemused expression on his face. "Yes?"

"I think this might take another night."

Jeremy blew out the breath he hadn't been aware he was holding. "You do, huh?"

"Oh yeah." Owen walked up behind him and placed one firm, possessive hand on his hip. "The whole weekend, maybe."

CHAPTER SEVEN

"Tasha, I told you I was fine."

"Honey, even over the phone, you're so bad at lying I almost feel sorry for you."

Jeremy chuckled, turning the wheel and guiding his truck down the dirt road that led to Owen's latest construction site. "It's been a weird week, that's all. Made all the harder by the secret your new protégé is making me keep. You want to tell me what you're doing inviting Jen to the club and letting her negotiate with strange men?"

"No, I do not. That's just between us girls. But I can fix any other problem you have. For example, I met someone this weekend and told him all about you. I think this one you might actually want more than once, my finicky friend. He's delicious. An architect with a head of blond hair, a lean body and a fetish for facial hair. Just your type."

Tasha's words made him flinch and he was grateful she couldn't see him. She would know right away that something had changed. The man he was on Wednesday was not the same man bringing his lover lunch on Tuesday.

His lover. Owen Finn.

He adjusted the Bluetooth in his ear. "I'm really not up for that kind of company. I have a lot on my plate right now. Anyway, I'd only disappoint him. The beard is gone."

"What?" He ducked his head instinctively at her shout of surprise. "Your beard is gone? You *shaved*? Did you lose a bet? And are you really telling me not to come over again? The way you did this weekend and last week?"

"No." Jeremy swore, slowing down as he drove past the crew decked out in hard hats, orange vests and tool belts. "Yes. Look, Tasha, I have to go but I'll call you later. I'm not brushing you off, honey, I promise. I just—"

"Oh my God, you're seeing someone, aren't you? As

in more than once, like a real live boy, seeing someone. Did you actually shave for *them*? Man or woman? Ooh, or is it a couple? *That* would keep you busy."

"Natasha—"

But she had the scent. "I have to go back to work, but if you don't answer the phone in two hours and tell me everything, I'm coming over and camping on your doorstep."

"I'll answer, I swear."

"See that you do."

On that ominous note, Jeremy ended the call and pulled up to the trailer that was the construction company's portable office. Grabbing the bag from Owen's favorite burger joint off the seat as he got out, he forced himself to look casual. He was having lunch with his friend. No big deal. He'd done it a thousand times before. Owen's crew knew him. They'd never suspect that something had changed.

The trailer door slammed open and Scott, Jen's fiancé, came stomping down the metal steps wearing an expression like a thundercloud. Hell. That couldn't be good.

Scott saw him and grimaced. "Hey, Porter."

Jeremy nodded as he passed, unwilling to start a

conversation that would delay him from seeing Owen. He was pathetic. The man had left his bed at dawn this morning and he was already impatient to see him again. Missing him as if he'd been gone for a week. He had to find a way to get a handle on this soon before they got careless and someone found out.

Just not yet.

When he opened the office door, Owen looked up from his paperwork, a snarl on his lips. Then he realized who it was and his expression relaxed. "Finally. Lock the door in case that idiot tries to come back in to give me another bullshit excuse."

Jeremy locked it and walked over to the small couch in the trailer, setting the food down on the coffee table before heading toward the mini fridge to grab a bottle of iced tea. "What's he done now?"

"Enough. I swear he'd be fired by now if Jen weren't marrying the bastard. He's incompetent, lazy and I hate to say it, but he stole from petty cash. Nothing drastic, but it's a little more than vending machine money. He says he used it to pay for the stripper so it was work related."

"That man is a walking cliché." He couldn't have drawn a more stereotypical douchebag.

"Tell me about it." Owen pushed back his chair and joined Jeremy on the couch before reaching for the food. "Thank you for this. I'm starving."

Jeremy watched Owen attack the burger with the same gusto he did everything else. He was a man with big appetites. Jeremy swallowed, trying to tamp down his arousal at the thought, and drank his tea in silence.

"Aren't you eating?" Owen asked between mouthfuls.

"Not hungry." He rubbed his hand over the back of his neck.

"What's wrong?"

Where to start?

"Tasha called. She's upset I've been avoiding her. She thinks I don't want her to bring her friend over because I'm seeing someone."

Owen's smile was dangerous. "She's always been the smart one. Is this a new friend or the moaner from the party?"

"New guy." Jeremy shrugged. "She knows I'm not into repeats."

"Then she doesn't know you as well as I do." He paused. "Or does she? That brings up an interesting question. Other than me, have you ever been with the same man for more than one night?"

This wasn't a comfortable conversation. "Rarely. I've had one or two weekends or four-day conventions with the same partner, but once the event was over? No."

"Huh," Owen grunted. "I had no idea comic book nerds were such sexual deviants. I would have taken you up on one of your invitations years ago. What about women? I'm excluding Natasha, of course."

"Same. You?" He didn't want to be the only one reciting his sexual resume.

Owen lifted one shoulder. "I have a few play partners I see once or twice a year who need more than cuddling after a session, but other than that, no."

Jeremy didn't like how that knowledge made him feel. So far Owen had been coming to him every night instead of going to the club, but how long would that last?

"What about that woman you were dating? Amy? Your brother Seamus seemed to think she had marriage potential."

Owen shook his head regretfully. "She was sweet. Nice. She also had a three-date minimum. If you made it to date four…" He shrugged. "Sadly, she was too nice and sweet to be a fan of date four. I'm not exactly her type."

They were a pair, Jeremy thought grimly. "So, we're *those* guys, huh?"

Owen frowned at him. "Those guys?"

"Those guys every good parent warns their children to avoid. The ones who don't do relationships." Guys who had sex partners instead of life partners. Who watched their previous conquests leave their beds and find someone else to spend the rest of their lives with. To be happy with.

Jeremy avoided Owen's penetrating stare. It wasn't flattering, but it was the truth. And depressing as hell.

"You turned her down." It wasn't a question. It was a command. And a grumpy one at that.

Jeremy looked back at him. "Tasha? Of course I did. You and I have an agreement."

Owen wiped his mouth with a napkin and reached for Jeremy's tea, finishing it off. "Right. Our agreement. I'm glad you weren't tempted to forget that, since we don't do relationships and we know how much you crave variety."

Why did he sound angry? After a few tense moments, Jeremy shifted, then stood and put his hands in his pockets, not knowing what else to do with them. "I should get going."

"Fine."

He turned to go with a frown. This was a new and uncomfortable feeling. As long as he'd known Owen, they could sit and talk—or not—for hours, and it was always comfortable. Now he didn't know what to say, or what he'd said wrong, and Owen wasn't helping. Why had he asked him to come in the first place?

He was reaching for the lock when Owen's hand shot out from behind him and landed on the door beside his head. Jeremy turned around, a question in his eyes.

"Jeremy, I..." Owen shook his head, and then he was kissing him, fingers digging hard into his scalp to hold him still while his mouth claimed Jeremy's in a fierce clash of tongues and teeth.

Yes, baby. I'm yours. Kiss me. Claim me.

Owen lifted his lips and swore. "I wanted you to bring lunch so I could prove to you that nothing had changed. That I could be in the same room with you and not lose control. That we could... Maybe this is still too new for that, because I can't stop imagining bending you over my desk and taking what I need."

They hadn't yet. Owen hadn't... "We can't. Not here."

"Not here," Owen agreed reluctantly. "I don't want anyone interrupting what I have in mind. But I'm damn tempted. I never got office fantasies until now. But with this? With you? I could take you so hard on that damn desk, Jeremy. I'd cover your mouth so no one could hear you scream and you'd love it."

Jesus, Owen was actually thinking about it. Jeremy could see the wheels turning in his mind as he weighed the possibility of getting caught against his lust. Time to do something to distract him before he forgot where he was and actually did it, and there was only one thing Jeremy knew would work on his insatiable lover.

His heart raced as he reached for Owen's belt, opening his jeans and gripping his velvet steel erection in his hand. Dropping to his knees, he parted his lips and swallowed the hard shaft down his throat. God, he loved the taste.

"*Jesus Christ*, Jeremy. Yes, oh yeah that's… You'd go down on me anywhere, wouldn't you? In your kitchen, in the alley, right here in the middle of the afternoon. Your mouth was made for this. For me."

He bent his knees and his hips started to pump aggressively against Jeremy's mouth. "I *am* going to fuck you," he muttered. "Maybe not here, but when I get home, I swear I'm going to remind you why you made that agreement with me in the first place. Why this is all you need and you'll come back again and again because you'll never get enough."

Neither one of them could seem to. Every time they were together now, they were on each other in minutes. It was a drug in his veins, Owen's reaction to him. Jeremy craved it. He reached up and cupped Owen's ball sac, caressing the tight skin as he gave his lover what he wanted.

"*Jeremy.*"

He felt Owen's climax fill his mouth and drank it greedily, so aroused it was all he could do not to join him. The only thing that stopped him was remembering all the men outside and the walk he had to make to his truck when this was over.

Owen shuddered as Jeremy licked the last drop from the head of his shaft before dropping to his own knees and kissing him again. It was sexy as hell, knowing he was tasting himself on Jeremy's tongue. He wanted to tumble him down to the floor and take him. Wanted to bend over his desk and beg to be taken.

Instead, he gently pulled away. "We should stop now. I might need a minute before I can walk in public."

"Damn." Owen was staring at him with worried eyes. "I'm sorry. I didn't plan on that. I mean I loved it, but I didn't bring you over here just to…"

He didn't want to admit how much he'd liked it. "I know you didn't. But plans change."

Owen's chuckle was raw. "Truer fucking words were never spoken." He stood and grimaced as he tucked himself back into his pants before helping Jeremy up. "I have an errand to run after work, but I'll be at your place as soon as I can. And I'll bring dinner."

Jeremy's throat tightened again. "Okay."

"And Porter?"

"Yes?"

Owen used his thumb to wipe Jeremy's lower lip. "When she calls back, tell Tasha you're in an exclusive relationship so you don't need her to find you any more men to play with. She won't leave you alone until you do. But don't mention me. I'm not ready for her to know just yet. Soon…but not yet."

Jeremy frowned. He hadn't expected Owen to want her to know at all, but still, the command left a knot in his stomach. "Thank you for your permission, Master Finn. I don't know what I'd do if you weren't around to give me orders."

Owen smiled. "You'd miss me. And you're going to spend the rest of the day thinking about me. About tonight."

He crossed his arms. "I don't know. I have a lot planned."

"Plan to get some rest," Owen advised softly. "You're going to need it."

Jeremy ran his hands through his hair and walked out of the trailer without saying goodbye, making a beeline for his truck. He needed to get out of here. Whenever he was with Owen lately he lost track of time, lost all perspective.

"Porter, hold up."

Scott. Great.

Jeremy wiped a hand across his face to make sure he was presentable without looking like he was making sure and then glanced at the brown-haired bruiser over the hood of his truck. "I have an appointment, Scott. Make it quick."

"I want you to tell that friend of yours to mind her own business," he blustered.

"*That* friend?"

"Jen's bridesmaid. Every time I turn around those two are together or talking on the phone."

Jeremy raised his brows. Someone was insecure. "She's trying to make sure Jennifer is really ready for your big day. Something everyone should be thinking about. No one wants to make a mistake."

The man's expression grew more belligerent. "You trying to say something?"

"No, son. If I was, you'd know it."

Scott started backing away. "You just tell her to stay away from Jen or I'll start talking about last Christmas. She'll know what I'm talking about."

Eyes narrowed, Jeremy started back around the truck toward Jen's idiot fiancé. Was he really going to pull this card? He obviously didn't know how dangerous Jeremy could be when someone fucked with his friends. "Last Christmas? Why would you want to admit to getting drunk and trying to force yourself on Natasha in the pub kitchen? I don't think Jen would be able to forgive that so easily."

Scott seemed surprised. "That's not what—I didn't force her. She saw mistletoe and came on to *me*."

Jeremy looked down on him, disgusted. "You're afraid she'll tell Jen about what you really did, aren't you? Natasha is too good a person to do that. She knows what the Finn brothers would do to you if they found out. What I was tempted to do as soon as she told me."

Scott's face twisted with bravado. "The Finn brothers. Like they can talk. They have everything they want and they'll still dip their wick into any woman with a pulse. That night is proof. I caught one of them taking a turn in their car with that bitch after she turned me down. She wasn't doing much to push him away either. It was a hell of a show."

Jeremy's fist tightened on Scott's collar until he started to choke and tried to bat him away. "You must be mistaken. And you really don't know when to stop talking, do you? All these years and you've never learned."

"Fuck you. You're just Owen's lapdog. You're no better than me, Porter. A stray dog they pity and teach to beg for scraps at their table. Only you actually think they're doing you a favor. You actually think you're family."

Jeremy lifted his fist in warning and Scott instantly held up his hands. "No, no, shit, I'm sorry, okay? I admit it, I didn't want Jen to know. I love her and I didn't want her to know."

Jeremy let him go and stepped back, noticing the other men had stopped working to watch them. Great.

Owen would know about the tussle before the day was over.

"I'm going to give you some advice, though I know you won't take it. If you really love her? You need to straighten the hell up and realize how lucky you are. You don't think it hurts her, the way you feel about her family? She believes you can be a good man, despite all evidence to the contrary, and she's stood by while you keep throwing her faith back in her face. Stop stealing, stop lying and try being worthy of your fiancée for once. If you don't, my new job is going to be making your life miserable. You've got it coming and I'll enjoy it."

He turned and walked around his truck, climbing into the driver's side and starting the engine before he looked up again. Scott was still there, rubbing his neck and glaring at him now that he thought there was a safe distance between them.

Jeremy rolled down his passenger side window and leaned toward it with a scowl. "Call me a dog again and I'll bury your bones where no one can find them." It was satisfying to see the man pale as he drove away.

Scott was a moron. The worst kind. He didn't know how good he had it. When Jeremy was younger, the only thing he'd wanted more than he wanted to draw was to be a member of the Finn family.

Of course, now there was something he wanted more than that. One thing. One Finn in particular.

"Hell."

CHAPTER EIGHT

His hands were covered in ink. Jeremy looked down at them and then over to the clock on the wall. He'd completely lost track of time. That hadn't happened in a while. Not with his contracted work anyway.

But this wasn't work. It was Owen.

Every sketch was of him. Jeremy studied the details in the eerily light blue irises, the way the eyes crinkled at the corners when he laughed. The strong jaw, as stubborn as it was handsome. Lips that could be firm in anger or soft in sensual wonder. He knew this face better than he knew his own. Had watched age and life experience define it. He knew all its expressions and moods, and he'd spent the last few hours capturing them all from memory, losing himself to each curve and line.

"Shit." This was bad. When had he gotten this pathetic? He wasn't a romance kind of guy, and God knew now would be the worst time to become one. Owen Finn was experimenting, he reminded himself for the hundredth time. The man was good at it and fucking thorough, but if Jeremy allowed himself to believe for one minute this could be more—he was just begging for heartbreak.

He never said he wanted it to be more.

He left his workroom and headed to the kitchen sink to wash his hands. Stubborn or not, Owen would surely come to the same realization that Jeremy had while thinking about the Finn family on the drive home. They were far too involved in each other's lives to keep this relationship secret for long. And while the brothers Finn might accept Owen—even congratulate him—for getting a woman to agree to being hog-tied and spanked for pleasure, it was highly doubtful they would be okay with his dating a man. And if they knew it was Jeremy, someone they considered an honorary part of the family? Their disapproval would mark the beginning of the end of his status with the Finn clan. He would be alone.

Even if was a short-term affair, if they found out they might never forgive him.

Tasha was the only other person in his life who was like family—which was why when she'd called back at the appointed time, he'd preempted her interrogation and demanded that she share the one detail about the Christmas party she'd previously neglected to mention. The one that worried him. The one having to do with a Finn in a car.

"I'm not going to tell you who, but I will admit that it happened," she'd offered carefully.

"*What* happened, Tasha? A kiss? A holiday cuddle?"

"Sex," she mumbled. "It was the only private place and believe me, I'm not planning on repeating it. Car sex is for teenagers."

Jeremy had laughed at that, but inside he was in knots. "Was it Owen, Tasha? You can tell me. You two have been dancing around each other for a while."

He couldn't believe how much it hurt to think it might have been him. But why would it matter? He and Tasha shared men all the time. He'd even wondered how long it would be before Owen suggested bringing her in as a third. He'd been preparing himself for it so he wouldn't react the way his confusing emotions might force him to—with jealousy.

"Not Owen," Tasha said firmly. "I know you tease

me about it a lot and I tell you about his women at the club, but I would never do that to you, Jeremy. I need you to know that."

Relief made him dizzy. "Me? What do you mean?"

"You *know* what I mean. And I've always known that was one line I would never cross. You're too good a friend." She paused. "Such a good friend that you're going to change topics, forget about my Finn fling and tell me who *you're* dating."

That distracted him. "I don't want to go into it yet, Tasha. It's too new. He's not... He's shy."

Tasha groaned in frustration. "He's shy. That's all you're going to give me? You shaved your beard for him and *he's shy?*"

"He makes me forget how to breathe." He could say that much and not give Owen away. "Makes me forget all the reasons I should hold back. He touches me and I'm willing to do anything he wants as long as he doesn't stop. As long as he stays."

"Well slap my ass and call me Lucy," she breathed. "You sound like you're falling."

He shifted uncomfortably. "Let's finish that sentence with *in lust*. I'm definitely falling in lust."

"Fine. I'll give your lusty lover another week to get

over his shyness and then I want to meet him. I promise I won't scare him away or suggest a threesome. Not until I know him better."

"You're a doll."

Tasha laughed at his arid tone. "I am! And I'm happy for you, Jeremy. You need some of this in your life. Someone who makes you feel like this. I'll tell you a secret. In our small menagerie of kinky, oversexed friends, I always thought you were the one who'd be happiest in a monogamous relationship."

"Really? The bisexual you like to have three-ways with? I'm the one who'd be happy with monogamy? You know I don't do that, Tasha. You're wrong. I'm not built for it."

"Yes you are," she insisted. "You have the right heart for it, and somewhere in that thick skull of yours you must know it, otherwise you wouldn't guard it so closely. When you really fall in love, it will be for keeps, and that is the scary, unadulterated truth." She paused. "I said almost the same thing to Seamus about Owen not too long ago. Leave it to me to befriend the two lustiest, relationship-phobic men on the planet."

Why was she mentioning Owen? Had she guessed? "Don't get ahead of yourself. I've only been seeing this guy for a few days, and I'm not planning on getting married anytime soon. I don't even have a dog. We should see if I can handle that kind of commitment first."

After they hung up, Jeremy had gone back to work, but now he went over the conversation again. A few things stuck out in his mind.

First, she'd slept with a Finn brother—and not the one who'd been playfully after her on and off since high school, but one of his siblings. Jeremy couldn't help but wonder how Owen would feel about that and if he should tell him. If they weren't together, he wouldn't be tempted. That was Tasha's story to tell, not his.

Then there was the fact that she'd turned Owen down all this time because of *him*. Somewhere, some part of him must have known that, but Jeremy was still surprised. Even when it seemed like an impossible crush, she'd silently been on his side. What would she say if she knew what Owen had asked for on his birthday? That he was the one Jeremy was hiding from her?

He hadn't kept the secret just because Owen told him to. He wasn't that far gone. He'd kept it because he was still pretty sure that other shoe was going to drop at any minute, and he didn't want her pity when Owen moved on, found the perfect woman for the Finn family to embrace and forgot all about that one short episode when he couldn't get enough of seeing Jeremy on his knees.

He looked around his house and sighed. This was a family home. The real estate agent had said as much. Sure, he'd turned one bedroom into a workout space and another into his office, but it was still too big to live in alone. He'd never thought so before. He'd relished the space, his room to breathe. His aunt's place had been the size of his bedroom closet. This house...well, it reminded him a little of the sprawling Finn homestead.

Now it all seemed excessive. It wasn't like he ever planned on having children, and not just because it was difficult to imagine finding someone he could spend the rest of his life with. His parents had screwed up his head by demanding a refund when their child didn't work the way they wanted him to. That was their legacy to him, and he didn't want to take the chance of passing it on.

He sighed. "Maybe I *should* get a dog."

Sliding open the patio door, he headed down the balcony stairs toward the water, thankful most of his neighbors were the holiday kind. The sun had gone down an hour ago, so even if they were visiting, they wouldn't be able to see much. He stripped as he walked out onto the dock and dived in without hesitation when he reached the edge.

The lake was the only place he ever felt at peace. It was the reason he'd bought this house. The water lapped against him in a soothing caress as he pushed himself a little deeper, a little farther out. Nothing could touch him here. Not his memories or his doubts. Not his fears about his feelings. He held his breath and let the water wash it away.

When the need for air forced him to break the surface, he felt the same small measure of release he always did. He started to backstroke lazily in the direction of the dock once more, tensing when he heard a splash behind him.

"This is *exactly* what I needed," Owen groaned. Jeremy turned in time to see him duck his head briefly under the water, the dim light from the dock glinting off his blond hair. "Damn, I love you for living by the lake. It's been one hell of a day."

Jeremy stayed where he was, his arms and legs easily keeping him afloat. "Oh yeah?"

Owen wiped one wet hand over his face before swimming closer. "Yeah. First, a few of the boys had issues with their paychecks, then our client decided that today was the day he was coming to inspect our progress with his wife—a woman who couldn't seem to understand why she had to wear a hardhat that would ruin her recent trip to the salon. And then, as you know, there was Scott..."

Shit. "What about him?"

"I heard he followed you to your truck and you seemed to be having a heated discussion," Owen admitted. "Unfortunately the jackass skipped out early and I didn't get the chance to interrogate him about it. Anything you want to tell me?"

Jeremy shook his head. "Nope."

"You know you're going to have to sooner or later."

"Just the usual bullshit." He wasn't going to touch this topic. He didn't want to risk mentioning Tasha's secret fling. "You know him."

Owen sighed. "Unfortunately. You know, I think he *wants* me to fire him? I don't get him, I really don't. He has the perfect girl, nepotism on his side at work, and my father and I bailing him out of all his small brushes with the law so Jen doesn't have to have her wedding in prison. Even you. He must have said something to get Mr. Still Waters to lose his temper. You'd think he'd be grateful we're so patient."

Jeremy studied Owen thoughtfully. "Stephen thinks you should stop bailing him out. So do I. He isn't grateful. He's resentful. He can't live up to any of you and he knows it. And if you ask me, I don't think Jen's entirely happy with the idea of spending the rest of her life stuck with him either, though she'll never admit it."

"I know it." Owen slapped the water with the palm of his hand. "Why the hell doesn't she call it off?"

"She's got a soft spot for wounded animals and broken toys." Jeremy watched the water glisten on his lover's shoulders, distracted by the way the light hit his skin. He wanted to draw that too. He sighed at himself in disgust, speaking without thinking. "There's also the Finn factor."

"The Finn factor?"

"Your family of success stories." Jeremy shrugged. "It's hard to measure up to. Your father started with nothing to build the family bar that's now a neighborhood institution. Your mother writes a successful series of children's books because she refused to let her dyslexia be a handicap. Your oldest brother Stephen became a damn fine state senator despite his rebellious youth, and his twin Seamus is raising four brilliant and well-loved children as a single parent, half of whom aren't biologically his. And then there is you. The All American quarterback who earned a full scholarship and started his own thriving business before his degree had time to get framed for the wall."

Owen splashed him. "Bah. We're lucky. A little more Irish than other people."

Jeremy smiled and pushed the water around with his hand before continuing. "Jen's Irish too. She's also the only girl in the family and the baby at that. I imagine she thinks she should have it all figured out by now, the way everyone else did at her age. But she doesn't. The only project she's ever had is good old Scott, with his rough childhood and his broken wings, and she doesn't want to admit it's a failure. That girl might be the smartest of the lot of you, but she's a stubborn Finn. She won't admit to being wrong without a fight."

Owen shook his head, his expression rueful. "I'm going to need you to write all that down so I can give this speech to Mom. Better yet, you do it. She listens to you."

Jeremy chuckled. "Jen is who you should be talking to. Her stubborn ways might get her into trouble if you don't."

Especially if Tasha turned her head by introducing her to the club. He really wished he hadn't promised not to tell Owen about that.

"What about you?" Owen asked, swimming around him with an enigmatic smile. "If you won't tell me what you and Scott talked about, tell me about the rest of your day. How was your afternoon?"

"Busy," Jeremy said, looking away from that knowing gaze. "I only just stopped working."

"I figured." He moved closer and reached up to touch Jeremy's cheek. "You have ink on your face."

"I do?" He tried to wipe it off but Owen took his hand, pulling him back toward the shore beside the dock.

"Just a smudge," Owen assured him. "It's cute. Nowhere near as bad as that time you came to Thanksgiving with a handprint on one side of your face. Stephen thought you were making a statement to draw attention to the plight of Native Americans, but I knew you'd just fallen asleep in the middle of doodling again."

He put his hand on the slope of grassy shoreline where he'd dumped his jeans and boots and dragged Jeremy closer. "Come back inside and I'll wash you off and feed you before I have my way with you."

Jeremy halfheartedly tugged his hand away. "I'm not

ready to go in yet."

"Yes, you are," Owen argued with a smile. "You've been ready since you left my office. You've thought about me all day, exactly like I told you to."

"You are so damn cocky, you know that?" Jeremy trapped him against the shore and his body, tangling their legs together. "I agreed not to be with other people while we're doing this, but that's it. You don't run my life. I didn't sign on to be your slave, Finn."

"Not yet."

Jeremy growled and kissed his lips with all the confusion, hunger and fire burning inside him.

Owen had been taking the lead sexually from the start, topping from the bottom, making him shave, finding a way to get him on his knees. And Jeremy kept following, unable to deny the chemistry or the way he felt when Owen took charge. He didn't know if it was a reaction to today or his nerves about what might happen tonight, but some part of him wanted to reassert his power over Owen. Wanted him to know he wasn't always going to get to be in control. He needed him to know that. He needed to believe that himself.

He lifted Owen up until his back was arched over the slope beside his clothes, his legs dangling in the water.

Then he followed, pressing their wet bodies together and kissing him with carnal intent.

Owen moaned, his arms around Jeremy's shoulders and his erection rocking against him. Jeremy knew the dock and the darkness wouldn't protect them completely from prying eyes, but he didn't want to stop. Couldn't stop when Owen was writhing under him and digging strong fingers into his back. For all his talk about control, the kinky bastard didn't mind having it taken away.

Owen turned his head, breaking the kiss to gasp, "Pocket. I have lube in my jeans pocket."

Jeremy's cock jerked and he reached out to fumble for the crumpled jeans. "Damn Boy Scout now? Always prepared?"

"I have to be with you around."

All the blood was rushing to his dick so fast he was dizzy. His hands trembled as he palmed the travel-sized bottle of lube and got to his knees. "Roll over, Owen."

The stubborn blond hesitated, taunting him. "Try and make me."

Jeremy felt another growl gathering in his chest. He wanted to play that game? He slid his hands under his lover's strong back and flipped him over forcefully, sitting on his thighs and holding his head down on the grass. "Try like this? Is this what you wanted?"

Owen inhaled sharply when Jeremy opened the lube with one hand and poured it out liberally, using his fingers to massage the tight hole he was desperate to slide into.

Jeremy rose up enough to force Owen's legs apart and kneel between them, pushing his thumb into the hot, perfect ass beneath him. "You had lunch," he rasped. "Had your fill and left me hungry. It's my turn."

"Yes," Owen whispered harshly. "Fuck, yes, Jeremy. Do it."

He leaned over and lowered his voice. "Do what? Forget about Master Finn's plans and fuck you right here in the dirt where anyone could see? Take you like an animal because I can't wait long enough to drag you inside?"

"Jesus," Owen moaned. "Yes, damn it. Right here."

Jeremy didn't need to be told twice. He tilted Owen's hips and spread his ass cheeks, lined himself up to thrust home...and then froze and started to swear. "Condom," he rasped. "Shit, I don't have a condom."

"Good," Owen responded breathlessly. "You don't need it. You're the only one I've let... I want to feel you inside me. Just you."

Jeremy was shuddering with the effort to hold himself back. He'd never been irresponsible. Never had sex without protection. But he couldn't deny that he wanted it with Owen. He didn't want anything between them either.

I want to feel you inside me. Just you.

"Fuck," he growled, pushing through the tight barrier and feeling the heat burn the head of his cock. "*Fuck*, Owen. Oh God, that's so good."

Owen's hands were clawing at the grass and his voice was thick with arousal. "Give it to me, Jeremy. Take what you want."

"Still a bossy bastard, even like this." Jeremy gripped his hair tighter with one hand and used the other to bend Owen's arm back behind him as he pressed his hips forward slowly. "Remember? You like this, don't you?"

"*Jeremy.*"

He dragged his hips back before thrusting deeper, still conscious of his size. He couldn't let go completely. No matter how many times they were together, he always tried to be careful.

"God," Owen choked out as if sensing his hesitation. "Don't go slow. I can take it. I need it. God, I love it."

Jeremy did too. Being inside Owen with nothing between them, holding him down and smelling the earth beneath them, he felt feral. Primal. He'd captured his prey and it was begging to be claimed. Begging to give him everything he wanted.

"Don't scream unless you want company," he demanded roughly, his hips starting to pound against Owen with enough force that he could hear the sound of their slapping flesh echoing off the water.

"No, I won't. I swear, Jeremy. Oh fuck you're— *Fuck!*"

"So tight, baby," he muttered, only partially aware he was talking out loud. "Your ass is gripping me so tight. Love fucking you. Gonna fuck you so hard."

Every sharp gasp and soft pained moan from Owen spurred him on. "Tell me you love it. Tell me you want more."

Don't make me stop.

"Yes." Owen's reply sounded strangled, as if he were struggling for breath. "Yes, Jeremy. God, yes."

He could feel his climax flying toward him but he couldn't stop long enough to reposition them so he could grip Owen's shaft. He wanted him to come, but he couldn't stop. He shifted and started to fuck him with deep, long hard strokes that made them both moan out loud.

"Owen, damn it, I'm close. You feel too good. I need to come inside you. Nothing between us. Jesus, coming so hard, I'm gonna to fill you up."

He bit off the shout that came with his orgasm, feeling the hot jets of release pumping out from his cock and into Owen's tight ass. Heaven. It felt like heaven.

Mine. You're mine now, Owen Finn. Please be mine.

"Jeremy!" Owen's surprised cry sounded loud in the darkness and he felt the body beneath him shaking. He let go of Owen's arm and bent down to kiss his back, his shoulders as both their bodies quake with their climaxes.

Jeremy breathed out in relief. He'd never been so selfish with a lover before, always seeing to their pleasure before his own, but Owen had pushed him over the edge. Thank God he'd come. "You okay?"

Jeremy moved off of him, caressing Owen's hip as he looked down at the results of his climax dripping down his lover's ass cheeks. It shouldn't be this satisfying to see, but he couldn't deny that it was. He felt like beating his damn chest, it felt so good. Or it would, if Owen would say something.

He needed to stop staring long enough to take care of

him. "Can you move? Do you want to go inside and shower now?"

In answer, Owen pushed himself to his feet, grabbing his clothes and walking a little unsteadily toward the house without looking back to see if Jeremy would follow.

Had he been too rough? Owen didn't do quiet. Especially when it came to sex.

Jeremy stood up, his stomach in knots as he strode after him, leaving his clothes on the dock in his impatience. "Owen?"

He followed him through the house and reached the bathroom in time to see his lover step beneath the shower spray. His heart sank. He *had* been too rough. Owen was always trying to push him to let go but he should have resisted. He knew better.

He'd let his passion get the better of him and he'd gone too far. "I'm sorry."

Owen opened his eyes and stared at him in silence for a minute before holding out his hand. Jeremy took it without stopping to think, hoping it meant he was forgiven. Or that he would be.

He sighed when Owen traced the ink on his cheek again, cupping his face and reaching up to kiss him softly. This wasn't the hungry attack he'd come to expect from his lover and friend. This was gentle. Achingly tender.

The hot water pounded against them as they explored each other's mouths with slow, sensual wonder. Jeremy let Owen take the lead, feeling vulnerable and exposed as he gave himself up to the kiss.

A thought came to him then and hit him hard enough to make his knees buckle, forcing him to lean back against the tile wall. No matter how logical he tried to be, or how certain he was that this wouldn't last, Jeremy was falling hard.

It hadn't been out of his way. He'd been half in love with his best friend for most of his life. He'd managed to keep it to himself for years, though not entirely. Tasha had known. Still no one else ever had to. Not even Owen. Especially not Owen.

Falling in love was the quickest way to ruin a friendship.

When you really fall in love, it will be for keeps...

Jesus, what was he going to do?

Jeremy lifted his head to see a smile that tore at his heart. In silence they washed each other's bodies, neither willing to shatter the fragile moment with words. He watched his soapy fingers massage the lean muscles of Owen's chest and stomach, felt them glide over tight butt cheeks and between as he tended to his lover.

It was the most intimate experience he'd ever had.

They rinsed off and stepped out of the shower, taking more time to carefully dry each other's bodies before Owen took his hand and guided him to the bed. He lay down in the middle and opened his arms and Jeremy didn't resist. He joined him, pressing his ear against Owen's chest and listening to his heart. It was a strong heart. A loyal heart.

It was a hopeless wish, but Jeremy wanted it to be his.

He wasn't sure how much time had gone by before Owen finally spoke. "I left our dinner sitting out on the kitchen counter. What do you say we warm it up and watch some television while we eat?"

Jeremy didn't want to move. He didn't want to talk about dinner. He wanted Owen to tell him how he was feeling, but that obviously wasn't an option. "Pizza again?"

"Yes," Owen laughed softly. "But I promise, I'll get Indian tomorrow. Unless you feel like breakfast for dinner, because you know that's all I can cook."

Jeremy pushed himself up and studied the light blue eyes he knew so well. "Tomorrow, huh? Is that your way of asking for an invitation?"

Owen rolled off the bed and walked over to Jeremy's dresser, opening a drawer and grabbing a pair of sweatpants. Jeremy kept his disappointment to himself when Owen slipped them on.

"Actually it is," Owen said as he tossed an extra pair at Jeremy. "But not for dinner. That rainstorm last night? It came in through the roof of my living room. That's why it took me so long to get here—I was arguing with my landlord."

"Shit, Owen, how long have I been telling you that whole complex should be condemned? I don't have to be in construction to know that."

"I know. But it's just a place to sleep. If I need more than that I have the family house, Seamus, here…" Owen shrugged. "The point is, it won't be livable for a week or so. I was thinking if I bribed you with your favorite food and promised not to steal the covers, you'd let me stay here until it's fixed."

"Like it's even a question." It never had been before. "Lord knows I have enough room."

No one in the family would think it was strange.

Owen stayed here all the time.

He stopped at the counter and looked at Jeremy over his shoulder with a smirk. "We just need the one bedroom, unless you're feeling adventurous. I won't be slumming on your couch."

The idea of having him here every night made Jeremy happier than he had a right to be. Hadn't he been thinking about how empty this house was? "Let's eat. Beer?"

"Of course."

They warmed up the pizza in the oven and carried it into the living room with a few bottles of beer. Jeremy picked one of their favorite movies to watch as they ate in companionable silence.

Owen snorted and reached for his beer. "That man is a badass."

He shook his head. "The raccoon is a badass. That man is his comic relief."

"They should make one of your comics into a movie."

Jeremy smiled. They'd had this conversation more than once. "Maybe they would if I drew more explosions."

Owen slapped his hand on Jeremy's thigh. "Which is

what I've been saying you needed all along. Explosions are cool."

"If you're thirteen," Jeremy countered, setting down his beer.

Owen followed his lead. "All men are thirteen, Jeremy. Inside where it counts. That's why you make the big bucks."

"I can't argue with that logic. Now stop talking and watch the movie."

Jeremy stiffened in momentary surprise when Owen wrapped an arm around his shoulder and pulled him back against the couch beside him. It felt good. Strange but familiar at the same time.

It didn't take long for him to lay his head on Owen's shoulder. For Owen's fingers to trace teasing designs against his shoulder. For Jeremy's hand to naturally land on Owen's thigh, squeezing the hard muscles he could feel through the loose-fitting sweatpants and moving higher.

He wasn't paying attention to the movie anymore. He closed his eyes and breathed Owen in. His skin smelled like Jeremy's soap, but his soap had never smelled so good on him. Like sex and sin and home.

He couldn't help but think about the way he'd lost

control outside. He'd been too turned on to stop, and it surprised him in more ways than one. He'd never been in a relationship with a man like this. He had sex, he moved on. If it was really good, he might save the phone number, but he always made sure everyone knew the score going in. It was the same with women, other than Natasha. She was his exception. Being with her was easy. No strings.

This had strings. Maybe not for Owen, but Jeremy could already feel them tangling up his thoughts and tugging at his heart.

Owen would be here for a week or more. Every night. Every morning. It was terrifying...how much he was looking forward to it.

CHAPTER NINE

The rain was pummeling the windshield so that even with the wipers on full speed, Jeremy could hardly see a foot in front of him as he slowly made his way home from the grocery store.

The foul weather had him grinning like an idiot. If anyone could see him they'd think he was crazy, but this storm meant Owen had the whole day off. It also meant that no one was working on fixing his apartment's roof, so he was stuck with Jeremy for the duration.

The last four days had been good. Better than good. Every day he woke up to Owen making breakfast and every night he fell asleep in his arms. He'd never experienced anything like it before. Never realized how much he craved the closeness, the intimacy, until now.

The night Owen had asked to stay for the week, they'd fallen asleep together on the couch, both too exhausted from their lakeside tussle to finish the evening the way the dominant Finn had planned. They'd woken up around two in the morning and shuffled down the hall to collapse together on the bed, neither moving until the alarm went off four hours later.

Owen had toned down his aggressive demands to top him, and he'd shied away from intercourse entirely since then. If he weren't so physically affectionate—always finding reasons to touch him when they talked—and if he hadn't made sure Jeremy came at least twice a night and most mornings, Jeremy would worry that Owen was regretting their time together and pulling away. As it was, Jeremy thought he might still be recovering from the rough sex by the water.

He would never stop kicking himself for losing control.

Even with his concern, this week was still better than any he'd had in a long damn time. They talked—not about movies or sex, but real conversations. Well, Jeremy talked—Owen listened and asked the occasional quiet question. But Jeremy cherished the time, telling him things he'd never been able to share with him before. Like the details of what had happened in the weeks leading up to his father handing him a wad of cash and warning him not to come back or ask for more.

He told Owen about the first time he'd had sex with a man. How he never would have worked up the nerve if Tasha hadn't dared him to do it. And he finally got Owen to share the story about the girlfriend in college who'd introduced him to the lifestyle.

When he'd asked him what drew him to it, Owen had opened up. He said it was the honesty. The lack of judgment and emotional manipulation. He liked that everything was spelled out in the kink community, said it taught him to rein in his tendency for excess and gave him patience. Taught him how much more enjoyable it could be to give pleasure than to receive it.

The way he talked about it made Jeremy see kink through new eyes. Curious eyes. He'd fought it when Owen got too bossy, and it tangled his stomach in knots when he thought about how easily he succumbed to the man's commanding ways. But Owen's conversations about power exchange made him realize that it wasn't a competition or a struggle for control. Submission wasn't a weakness.

Last night, after the rain started, Jeremy had been in

Owen's arms and he'd wondered out loud if they could do a little more experimenting. Owen had tensed beside him and then pulled him closer, pressing a kiss to his forehead.

"Tomorrow."

Today, Jeremy thought, his hands tightening on the steering wheel as his back wheels skidded on the wet surface of the road. Today he was going to give in to his own curiosity, and he was determined to do it with the same fearlessness Owen had shown on his birthday.

He didn't know if what they were doing would last beyond Owen's roof getting patched. He hoped, but with all their talking they'd never mentioned anything about the future. Jeremy didn't want to waste a minute or have a single regret. He loved Owen, and wanted to know every part of him, including Master Finn.

When he finally pulled into the driveway and shut off the engine, Owen was already striding out the front door and drenched to the bone as he came to help him unload the supplies. Water and candles, canned goods and propane for the grill in case the power went out.

"How are the roads?"

Jeremy grimaced. "Not good. I'm glad I went out when I did. I doubt they'll be drivable until this is over.

Do we still have power?"

"For the moment. Come on, let's get inside."

He shivered when he stepped into the air-conditioned foyer, water streaming from his hair down into his eyes as he headed to the kitchen with his bags. "I'm sorry it took me so long to get back. Traffic was slowed to a crawl."

Owen set his handful of bags on the counter. "That's okay. It gave me time to get ready."

Jeremy pushed his wet hair back from his forehead and met Owen's gaze. His heart started hammering in his ears. "Ready?"

"Let's get this put away first."

He was clumsy, suddenly all thumbs and shaking hands as they put away the groceries and supplies in silence. He'd asked for this. He wanted it. But when he glanced up toward the living room, he lost his breath.

Owen *had* been getting ready. He'd moved all the furniture up against the wall and out of the way. He'd also brought out a flat padded bench from the workout room.

What was he going to do to him on that bench? Jeremy's dick pressed insistently against his jeans and he licked his dry lips. What kind of torture was Owen planning?

A hand covered his and took the can he'd been holding away from him. "That's the last one," Owen murmured. "Now let's take off your clothes so we can put them in the washer."

Jeremy pulled off his wet t-shirt while Owen unbuttoned his jeans. He kicked off his boots, leaning over to pull off his damp socks before shucking off the clinging denim. Owen gathered his clothes and disappeared into the laundry room for a moment, leaving him standing naked and trembling in his kitchen.

He glanced at the refrigerator. Had it only been ten days since he'd leaned against it and Owen had talked him into opening his pants out of curiosity? How could his life have changed so completely in less than two weeks?

When Owen reappeared he was barefoot and shirtless, but he still had his pants on. He studied Jeremy's body as if he were seeing it for the first time, lingering on the thick erection between his legs.

He held out his hand. "It's tomorrow, Jeremy. Are you ready for this?"

"I think so." He took Owen's hand and let him lead him into the living room. "I like your decorating style."

Owen laughed. "I had to work with what we had on hand, but we needed the space." His thumb caressed Jeremy's palm. "I'm going to start out simple. Some teasing and touching while you're cuffed to the bench. We'll go from there."

He was so busy staring at the bench and the black suede-and-leather cuffs lying on either end that it took him a moment to notice the television was on. An aroused, naked man was standing in his living room beside a workout bench and his lover.

His eyes narrowed in on the camera attached to his large screen. "Owen? What the hell is that?"

"I want you to be able to see everything I'm doing to you. You're an artist and a man. I thought you'd appreciate the visual."

Jeremy swallowed. He wasn't wrong. "Is it recording?"

The hand holding his tightened. "Let's leave that a mystery for the moment. I like the idea of you wondering whether or not your screams of pleasure will be saved for posterity, or if they're being sent out on a live feed for anyone with an Internet connection to see."

Jeremy shook his head. He knew from their discussions that Owen would never expose him that way without negotiating it in advance, but the suggestion definitely fucked with his head. If he didn't trust him so much… "That's evil."

"Welcome to my world. Now I want you to kneel in front of the bench and spread your arms out on either side."

He did as Owen asked, stretching his arms out on the bench so his wrists and part of his forearms were hanging off both ends. Owen knelt down beside him and reached for the first cuff. It had a chain attached to it that went underneath the bench to attach to the cuff on the other side.

Oh God.

It felt soft, he thought as Owen fastened it to his wrist. Still firm, but softer than he'd imagined it would. "Have you used these before?"

"You're wrists are thicker than my usual partners'," Owen offered with a slight smile, moving to the other side of the bench. "A few days ago I stopped to get some things on the chance you might be willing. The cute little salesclerk was very helpful with one purchase in particular."

"What purchase?" Jeremy flexed his cuffed hand, watching Owen's every move.

When he was done with the other cuff, Owen got up and walked over to the coffee table that he'd slid against the wall. He picked up a large white towel that was bundled there, carrying it over and setting it down on the floor for Jeremy's inspection. Spreading out the towel, he started arranging the objects that had been hidden inside. There was a new bottle of lubricant, a sixteen-inch paddle made of black leather and—

Jeremy's eyes widened when Owen picked up a bright red anal wand. "You're fucking kidding me."

Owen smiled, pleased with himself. "You like it? She said this was a good one. You're lucky she was around, too, because my first instinct was…well, she seemed to think you would run screaming in the other direction."

The plug was the only toy Jeremy had ever used, and before Owen he'd done that alone. He'd never had anything like *that* inside him. It was long with eight round beads, each one thicker than the last. "Owen…"

Light blue eyes narrowed on him. "*Jeremy?* Backing down already?"

No. No, he could do this. He wanted to do this. "Do I get a safe word?" he joked weakly.

"Yellow," Owen answered immediately, his expression letting Jeremy know exactly why he'd chosen it.

He glared at the cocky blond. He wasn't scared. He looked at the wand again, then the paddle. Maybe he was cautious. It would be strange if he weren't. But there was excitement mixed in with the wariness. Impatience. "What happens now?"

The set of Owen's shoulders relaxed, and Jeremy realized he hadn't been sure of his response. *Not so cocky, after all*, he thought, biting his cheek to keep from smiling. It was nice to know.

"This." Owen kissed him, tangling his fingers into Jeremy's hair and tugging in a way that made his cock jerk. Jeremy tried to reach for him but the chain went taut, limiting his movement.

Owen pulled back with a smile. "Not this time, Tarzan. I'm in control now."

His hand skimmed down Jeremy's spine, making him shiver. "I can touch you wherever I want, however I want, and all you can do is accept. Put yourself in my hands."

Owen touched him. Tickled his sides, pinched his nipples until he flinched. He traced his ribcage with short nails and rubbed the tension out of his shoulders. Whenever Jeremy lost focus, he would reach up and pull his hair again. Hard.

It was incredible.

His palm was hot on Jeremy's hip and he squeezed before reaching for the lube and the wand. "You're doing so well, Jeremy. Now you have to trust me more than you ever have before. The way I trust you."

Still on his knees, Owen moved until he was beside Jeremy's hip, one hand firmly on his lower back. He paused long enough that Jeremy looked up at the television screen. Owen's expression as he stared at the body beside him was gratifying.

"Like what you see, Master Finn?"

"Oh yeah." Owen's low groan sent a jolt of hard pleasure through his body. "Fuckable art," he murmured, reminding Jeremy of that first night. "Are your eyes on the screen, Jeremy?"

"Yes."

His tone hardened. "Keep them there and don't move unless I tell you to."

He could hear the wet sounds of Owen lubricating the wand, and then he felt the cool liquid between the cheeks of his ass and Owen's fingers massaging and pressing against his sphincter. *Oh God*, he thought, biting his cheek hard. *Oh God, he's really going to do this.*

The stinging smack of a palm on his ass cheek made Jeremy flinch. His skin warmed, then heated when Owen landed a few more blows in the exact same spot. His mouth opened in surprise when he felt Owen's teeth and the swipe of his tongue there as well, intensifying the sensations. What was he doing? That felt... "Jesus."

"Watch me, Jeremy," Owen commanded, using one hand to spread his ass as the other guided the tip of the wand to his tight hole. "Watch me while I'm watching this."

He knew from the moment the first smooth, round bead pushed inside him that he wouldn't be able to obey. But he tried. He saw Owen guiding the wand into his ass. He'd gotten it for the sole purpose of using it on him. Fucking him.

Whatever you want, Owen. Don't stop.

The next bead stretched him and popped inside and he clenched his fists.

Deeper, baby. Go deeper.

Owen dragged it back slowly before pushing it inside again and adding the third, thicker bead.

"Oh God," Jeremy moaned softly.

"Is something exciting happening on the screen?" Owen's voice was deep. Distracted. "I don't know if it can top this show. I can't take my eyes off your ass. I want to see how much it can take."

Jeremy had to breathe out forcefully when the fourth knob slid inside and then out as Owen pulled the wand back again. He started to fuck him with it like that, just the first four beads, in and out in shallow thrusts.

He was teasing Jeremy, knowing he was waiting for the rest. Jeremy pushed his hips back when Owen thrust again, taking in the fifth bead with a groan. "Fuck."

Owen spanked him in that spot, the spot that still tingled. "Did I tell you to move?"

"No."

Owen's palm landed again and again at the same time he was thrusting the sixth and seventh beads inside Jeremy's ass.

"Owen!" Jeremy screamed. "Fuck, that's…"

"That's nothing, Jeremy." He started to shaft him with the wand in long, slow strokes. His expression on the screen was focused, his cheeks flushed. "You can take it if I can. This isn't anything compared to being stuffed with your monster cock. Pressed into the ground and hammered until you aren't sure you'll be able to stay conscious."

"I'm sorry," Jeremy gasped, tilting his hips to accept

his punishment. God, it felt good. "I told you I was sorry, Owen."

Owen bit his shoulder hard, reaching underneath Jeremy with his free hand and wrapping a fist around his erection. "You should be sorry. You probably will be. Do you know why?"

Jeremy shook his head, grunting when Owen pushed the eighth bead—*so fucking big*—inside his ass.

"Because I loved it," he whispered, pausing to let Jeremy adjust to the fullness. "I shouldn't have. You took away all my control and fucked me so hard I walked with a limp the next day, but I loved it. I was right about you and primal play, Jeremy. I just didn't think about how hot it would make *me* to be your prey."

"Jesus, Owen."

He started dragging the wand back slowly, one bead at a time. So damn slow. "I came in the dirt like a hard-up kid and realized that everything I believed about myself had shifted. I'm an open-minded guy. I'm about pleasure, not labels. But I never thought I was a *catcher*, either, Jeremy. Not until you. Even now, when I've got you trussed up and completely under my control, I want it again. I'll be honest, it's been messing with my head."

"So this is payback?" Jeremy gasped out when only

the last, small bead remained inside him and Owen was gripping the base of his shaft tight. "Not that I mind. It *is* your turn."

"This is pleasure, Jeremy. This is us. I'm a little competitive, I admit that. But you are too." He removed the wand and set it on the towel. "You're also as curious as I am. You've been wondering about my paddle since I brought it up that first night. Wondering if you'd enjoy what I can do to you as much as I've loved what you've done to me."

It was true, but Jeremy wasn't ready to admit it out loud. "A *little* competitive?"

Owen chuckled, standing to remove his pants before going for the leather paddle. "I'm compensating. Anyone but an over-endowed porn star would be with that *Boogie Nights* prop you're always swinging around. At least I'm man enough to admit it."

Jeremy grinned despite his arousal, studying the body towering over him. "You have *nothing* to be ashamed of."

Owen's erection looked so good it made his mouth water. He wanted to taste it again. Wanted to hear his lover cry out his name and feel his hands in his hair.

"I plan on proving that to you later." Owen looked

down at him and his smile turned wicked. "But now I'm going to use this on your tattooed ass. I decided to skip the hard wood and go for leather for your first time."

Was that supposed to ease his mind? "Now? You're not going to…finish?"

"You mean let you come?" Owen responded, a sadistic glint in his eye. "Are you close, Jeremy?"

"Hell yeah."

"Look at the screen. Now."

He did, hoping he would see Owen kneeling down beside him again. Touching him until he found release. Instead Owen stayed on his feet, raised the hand holding the black paddle slightly and brought it down with surprising force on Jeremy's ass.

"Damn it, Owen. Fuck."

"Did that hurt?"

"Yes!"

He did it again, his aim landing the middle of the paddle on one ass cheek, then the other. His hand followed, a tender touch tracing the stinging flesh and making Jeremy tremble. "Breathe, Jeremy."

He hadn't realized he'd been holding his breath. His skin was hot, but it didn't hurt as much as he'd thought it would after the first blow. And Owen's touch was a soothing balm. He pressed against the hand, wanting more.

The paddle returned instead. At first it was slow but firm, almost hypnotic. When his skin began to buzz with sensation, Owen started beating a fast staccato rhythm on his ass that made him cry out in surprise.

"Don't get too comfortable," Owen commanded. "Let yourself feel the fire and the vibration of it going through you. Like it, even if you think you shouldn't. Let go and watch me."

Jeremy watched the screen through his damp eyelashes, seeing one man bound and another wielding a paddle in one hand and a soothing caress in the other. Pleasure and pain. Over and over it repeated until he wasn't sure what he was feeling, only that Owen was responsible for all of it. He had the control in his hands.

His breath came out like a sob as he let go and started calling Owen's name with every blow. He wanted him. Loved him. Wanted to please him. "Owen!"

The man on screen dropped the paddle and Jeremy felt Owen bend over him, felt his lips gently parting over his burning skin and his hands smoothing over his hips and thighs.

"So hot," Owen muttered. "You're responding so

well I almost forgot it was your first time."

Kiss me, Owen. Touch me. Need you.

"I need you," Jeremy whispered. "Please."

The fingers on his hips tensed. "Like this? Chained up after I've taken a paddle to your ass?"

Jeremy moaned. "Yes."

He felt Owen's body shudder against him. Then he heard the sound of the bottle of lube being opened again.

Yes. Take me. Only you, Owen. Need you.

Owen's fingers spread his ass cheeks and Jeremy flinched, hissing out a pained breath, but he didn't tell him to stop. He pressed his forehead into the bench and spread his knees farther apart to brace himself.

"Fuck, Jeremy," Owen muttered raggedly. He bent his knees and filled him with a steady, unyielding pace that drove Jeremy wild. It seemed to go on and on, his lover stretching him, owning him with his thick erection. This was Owen. Owen pushing through his tight, resistant flesh until, with one more powerful thrust, he was all the way inside. His hips pressed against him and Jeremy heard him groaning low in his throat. "*Yes.*"

"Oh God, Owen!" The chains jangled loudly as his whole body shook with an overload of sensation. Pleasure and pain. His skin was on fire but the feeling of

Owen inside him—he couldn't describe it. He needed him to move. "Owen, please."

Owen's body curved over his back, one hand lifting to grip Jeremy's shoulder. "Jesus, look at us. Look at us, Jeremy."

Through blurred vision he saw the erotic tableau. Blond and dark. Lean and large. Day and night entwined together, both reaching for something. Desperate for more.

Owen started moaning as he thrust inside him, deep long strokes that made Jeremy see stars instead of their reflection. "You feel so good," he groaned. "Tight and hot and *God*, it feels like I've waited forever to feel this. To be inside you. Fuck, *finally*. I can't believe you lasted as long as you did without a condom. I never want to put one on again."

Jeremy was all nerve endings and sensations. He couldn't think. Couldn't breathe.

Breathe.

"Hard."

"What did you say, Jeremy?"

"Harder, please."

Owen's hips responded instantly to the request, powering against him. "Like that?" The hand on his shoulder lifted and tangled in Jeremy's hair, yanking roughly until he was forced to tilt his head back. Tingling electricity shot up Jeremy's spine at the action. "You want a hard fucking? Want me to pound *your* ass for a change?"

"Please," he gasped. "Please, Owen."

"If I didn't need it so bad, I'd make you wait. Drive you crazy. But you're too good, Jeremy. It's never been this—*God, yes!*"

There were no more words as Owen took him with a ferocity that might have surprised Jeremy if he wasn't so lost in his own pleasure.

Love you, baby. Love you inside me. Love you so much.

Owen groaned, his hands clenching tight in Jeremy's hair. "I'm coming. I can't wait—*Jesus*, I can't—*Jeremy.*"

He could feel the hot spurts of Owen's climax filling his ass, loved the stretch as his cock kept pumping inside him as if it couldn't bear to stop. Then Owen's hand was on him, stroking the erection that was so hard it hurt, sliding up and down until he came with a shout that rattled the storm-soaked windows.

Dark spots filled his vision and he started to shake.

He didn't know which end was up or what he was feeling. It was too much. He couldn't control it.

"I'm here, Jeremy. I've got you." Owen's hushed words calmed him, and his gentle hands felt like they were the only things tethering him to the wildly spinning earth.

When he pulled him into his arms, Jeremy realized Owen must have taken the cuffs off. When he laid him on the bed—how had they gotten to the bedroom?—he rolled on his side and watched Owen disappear into the bathroom.

He came back with a cool, wet washcloth, lying beside Jeremy and gliding the cloth over his shoulders, his back, the tender cheeks of his ass.

"That's nice," he whispered, staring at the pulse beating at the base of Owen's throat. He felt a bit like he did the one time he got high at Comic-Con. "When Tasha talked about it, I always thought aftercare sounded strange. But that's what this is, right? You're taking care of me."

Owen's lips tilted in amusement and he nodded. "Yes I am. You deserve to be taken care of, Jeremy. You never ask for it, but I don't think I know anyone who deserves it more. You gave me a gift today. Gave me everything I asked for. It was so good I'm already planning on doing it again. But right now it's all about you. See how nice it can be when you let someone stick around after?"

"I can't believe we did that."

"Which part?"

Any of it. Jeremy couldn't believe any of it. Not one day since Owen's birthday. A wave of vulnerability washed over him. Was Owen going to leave now that he'd made sure Jeremy would never be satisfied with anyone else? Was their friendship going to follow him out the door, too shattered by everything they'd done to ever be the same?

Will he break my heart? Does he want more than sex?

Calloused fingers gripped his chin and lifted until he was looking into Owen's light blue eyes. "Where'd you go? Talk to me. I need to know how you're feeling. The drop can be pretty steep after that adrenaline rush."

Jeremy shook his head. "I'm fine."

"You can't fool me, Jeremy. I know there's something going on up there."

"Just a question." He reached up and placed his hand on Owen's bare hip, needing to touch him. Needing to distract him and desperate to lighten the mood. "Would it be gay if I asked you to hold me?"

Owen's surprised laughter fell on him like drops of unadulterated sunshine. He pulled Jeremy into his arms, still chuckling. "I'll hold you as long as you need me to, joker. I'm not going anywhere."

God, he wished that were true.

CHAPTER TEN

It had been two days and Jeremy could still feel the fading marks on his ass as he walked toward his front door. Running errands today, it had taken all his concentration not to get an erection in public each time he was reminded of what they'd done. He wished Owen hadn't phoned him at lunch to tell him he would be late. He wanted to thank him properly for his day of frustration. He wanted him home.

Home. Damned if he didn't like the sound of that. He'd been thinking about offering a more long-term living arrangement. Maybe under the guise of helping him look for a better place to live. Owen could stay here with him until he found someplace better.

If it were up to Jeremy, he would realize there was no

better place. He would stay. To the world outside they could be roommates and best friends. Inside the safety of their four walls? Owen would be his.

It was a good dream. One Jeremy found himself coming back to more and more often lately.

He heard Tasha crying an instant before he saw her leaning against his front door. "Natasha? Jesus, honey what's wrong?"

She turned and fell into his arms, sobbing. Jeremy unlocked and opened the door, picking her up easily and carrying her inside before kicking it closed behind them. "Come on, Tash, talk to me. Are you hurt?"

He walked over to the couch and sat down with her in his lap, crooning and rocking her as if she were a child. He'd never seen her like this.

She lifted her head and his heart broke. Her beautiful green eyes were red and swollen. She'd been crying for a while. "I'm going to kill him."

"I'll get my shovel and a good lawyer," he assured her solemnly without missing a beat. "Can you tell me about it? Who are we talking about?"

Tasha looked down at her hands, her dark velvet curls hiding half her face from view. "It's all my fault. I still can't believe it's really happening. I mean, this is

Lifetime movie bullshit, right? This isn't real life."

"Why don't you start at the beginning of the movie, hon. I'm lost."

She nodded. "Last night I went to the pub to talk to Jen about…well, it wasn't a PG-rated topic."

Jeremy nodded, caressing her back. "It never is."

"I didn't realize he was there, that he'd heard anything, but he must have, because he dragged Jen in the back and everyone could hear them shouting at each other until Seamus followed them to kick the bastard out and ban him from the pub."

Scott. She was talking about Scott. "He's going to have to be dealt with," Jeremy sighed. "I think I'm calling the Finns in for a meeting. We can't keep pretending we're okay with Jen marrying that asshole."

Tasha looked into his eyes, her own dark with worry. "No, we can't now. You can't. I'm so sorry, Jeremy. This is all my fault."

"Why are you sorry? You're starting to scare me now. Tell me what's going on."

She fumbled for the purse that was dangling from her shoulders, reaching in to dig out her phone. "I got a text message a few hours ago. There was a video and a picture attached."

Tasha pushed play and tilted her phone toward Jeremy. It was dark inside the car, but he could clearly see a topless Tasha, her expression passionate as she straddled the man whose face was buried in her lush breasts.

The Finn brother whose name she wouldn't reveal the last time they'd spoken. Even though they were twins, all it took was one look at the expensive if rumpled suit to know which one she was riding. "Stephen? You had sex with *Senator Finn* in a public parking lot?"

Stephen. The man whose career could be, if not ruined, then severely damaged by a sex tape. The public wouldn't care that they were both single, consenting adults. It would be a scandal. "Shit. You don't have to kill Scott. I will."

She stopped the video and took a breath. "I'm sorry, Jeremy."

"For that? Babe, you and I have done much w—"

"No," she interrupted. "I'm sorry for this."

Natasha opened an attached picture and he felt his heart stop then start to race so hard he thought it might explode. How? "Christ."

This morning he'd walked Owen to the door in

nothing but a pair of sweatpants. Owen been teasing him all through breakfast and Jeremy had wanted to make sure the fiend was just as affected for the rest of the day as he was going to be. He'd pushed him against the side of the house and kissed him with all the desire he was feeling. A desire that was meant for Owen alone.

And Scott had been there, watching. He'd snapped a fucking picture on his phone.

"Does he want money?" Jeremy asked grimly. He felt like the walls were closing in on him. Like his world might collapse. "Did he tell you how much?"

Neither of these could ever see the light of day. No one could know.

Tasha was soothing him now, her hands cupping his face. "If I could go back I would make better decisions. I wouldn't have given in to Stephen that night. I wouldn't have tried to show Jen that good a time. I wouldn't have taunted him, not if I thought for one second it would endanger your relationship with Owen. He's the one, isn't he? That's why you couldn't tell me."

"Stephen is who we should worry about," Jeremy said, lifting her off his lap and standing, because he felt the need to fight. "I've got money, Tasha. I'll make a deal w—"

"He didn't just send it to me," she interrupted him in a hushed voice that sounded like a shout to his ears. "He sent that text to four people simultaneously. Me, Stephen, Seamus…and Owen."

Jeremy swayed as if he'd been punched in the gut, the blood rushing in his ears in a deafening roar. The Finn brothers. All of them had seen him kissing Owen. Seen Owen kissing him back. "Jesus."

His legs gave out and he sat down heavily on his coffee table, feeling the ache from Owen's paddle and knowing he would never get that again. Never touch him again. Not now that they all knew. He reached for his own phone, his hands shaking so hard she could see it, and dialed Owen's number, listening to the ring while Tasha watched.

It went to voicemail and he hung up. "Damn it."

Tasha reached out, her hands on his knees. "Stephen called me right before I got here. He said they were all together and they would take care of it, but I—*we*—needed to stay away until they did. Finn business, he said."

Finn business. Not his business, but about him. God, Owen. What was he going through? Jeremy wanted to be at his side, to support him and defend him when he faced his brothers, but he knew Owen wouldn't welcome that.

It was all his fault. He shouldn't have kissed him outside where anyone could see. He should've been more careful. No one was supposed to know.

He looked at Tasha, feeling like he was drowning. "God, Tasha, what should I do? What am I going to do?"

For the first time he saw something that looked like pity in her eyes. "All we can do is wait, honey. We don't want Scott sending those to a gossip magazine or a news outlet. Stephen is good at this dance. He'll know how to play this game better than we ever could."

Stephen. Jesus. Stephen knew.

He focused on Tasha to distract him from his own suffering. "Are you finally going to talk to me now that the secret is out? You may as well, right? You know mine. Was that the first time you two were together? Because it didn't look like it."

Talk to me. Talk to me so I don't think about Owen.

Tasha leaned back on the couch, wiping her eyes. "Can't a girl get a drink before she starts swapping sex stories?"

He stood up and forced his legs to move to the kitchen, grabbing the bottle of tequila and taking a slug before handing it to her. "Drink."

She did, gasping a little and handing it back. "You're right, that wasn't the first time. The first time I was a freshman in college and he was in his fourth year."

"You mean *we* were freshman." He paused, remembering. "Wait, is that the older guy you were skipping classes for and being secretive about? The one who—"

"Yes," she cut him off, glaring. "That's the guy."

"And since then?"

Her fingers pressed against her temples. "Since then we've gotten together every few years. Sometimes for a half hour in a broom closet or a damn car, once or twice for an entire weekend. It varies."

"Every few years? Since *college*? Tasha, how could you keep this from me for so long? You tell me everything, even when I didn't want to know. And Owen—hell, you could have saved him years of lusting after you with a few words. The Finns don't go after their brothers' girls."

The Finns protected their own. Finn business. He was shut out from that now and Owen wasn't answering his phone.

Tasha's chuckle held no humor. "I'm not Senator Stephen Finn's girl. I never was. He was already on his do-good path to politics by then, remember? He had very definite ideas about where he was going and how he was going to get there. I was, and am, just a reminder of his good old bad boy days. A kinky itch he needs to scratch before he puts on his super suit to kiss hands and shake babies."

She shook her head, laughing again. "I mean, come on, Jeremy. Can you even imagine me as a politician's girlfriend? The headlines would write themselves. Ravenous Rivera's Three-Way Weekend. Notorious Natasha Gets Whipped at Fetish Club While Boyfriend Cuts Ribbon on New Hospital Wing." She snorted and reached for the bottle again. "And those would be the tame articles. Stephen can be a bit of a hypocrite, but I like him—I love *all* the Finns—too much for that."

Jeremy accepted the bottle when she was done, needing the tequila to soothe his frazzled nerves. He loved them too. That hadn't stopped him from destroying everything by being careless. "Does he know about us? You and me?"

"Of course. He also knows how important you are to me. And to Owen."

Owen.

"I think my Finn stock is plummeting as we speak."

He covered his mouth, as if he could hold back the emotions going through him. "He's never going to want to see me again. Fuck. None of them are."

They'd send him away, just like his parents. Only this would be so much worse.

"That's crazy, Jeremy. You're not thinking straight. They love you, honey. And if Owen doesn't tell you so himself, he isn't the man I've been friends with all these years. I saw his face when you kissed him. That feeling isn't something you give up on at the first sign of trouble."

Jeremy buried his face in his hands. "He was just curious," he whispered. "He never said... He never says anything like that. He loves the sex—wanted the sex— but that was all it was. We aren't together. We're not in love. You can't even call what we were doing dating. Not really."

He'd never said anything about them having a future. Never said anything about caring for Jeremy or wanting more from him then friendship and fucking. Jeremy thought...the way he acted...but Owen never said.

"Oh my beautiful man," Tasha said, her voice wavering. "You know I adore you and I'd do anything for you, but I won't let you lie to yourself. You might not be sure about how he feels, but *you're* in love with him. For the first time in your life you are head over heels and I messed it up. Some friend I turned out to be."

He reached for her and moved until they were lying on the couch together, her head on his chest. "You're not responsible for this, Tasha. Scott is. I hope like hell Stephen puts him in his place."

But even if he did, Owen would still have to face his brothers without him and explain that kiss. What would he say? That it was nothing? That it *meant* nothing?

"Damn it, I feel fucking helpless." Every instinct he had was telling him to go, to help. The only thing stopping him was the knowledge that his presence would make the situation worse.

"Jeremy? Can I stay here for a while?" The vulnerability in Tasha's voice had him tightening his arms around her. "I don't think you should be alone right now and I sure as hell don't want to be. I know you might hate me, but just for now can we pretend you don't?"

She was hurting. He had to get over himself and think about her. She needed him. She loved him no matter who he kissed. Who he loved. "Natasha, I love you as much as I always have. You can stay as long as you need to. We'll cuddle on the couch and I'll make your favorite pasta and we'll shut out the rest of the world. I think I have another tequila bottle in the cabinet. And vodka if we run out."

Tasha sighed, nuzzling against him. "You're the best friend a girl could have, you know that, right?"

His hand slid down her back and squeezed her ass. "You're not so bad yourself."

"Don't tease me." There was a smile in her voice at last. "I still have a crush on your body."

"Ditto, honey. You've ruined me for all other women."

She laughed, but it still sounded heavy with tears. "I don't think I'm the one who did that."

They spent the next few hours comforting each other before he started the coffee and made sure she ate. He knew they'd both come to some sort of unspoken understanding that the sexual aspect of their friendship was over. Too much had been revealed today—Jeremy's love for Owen and Tasha's conflicted emotions about Stephen.

He wished she'd told him about Stephen years ago. The uptight Finn brother now looked human in a way he never had before. And flawed. Now that Jeremy knew, he could see it in her face whenever she talked about him. Her feelings for Stephen were complicated but strong. There was more there than she was saying. He also had a feeling the casual nature of their relationship wasn't entirely her choice. What was wrong with Stephen? Why did he keep stringing her along?

Damn those Finn boys for being oblivious and stubborn and impossible to resist. Damn them for only wanting sex and refusing to give their hearts in return.

Natasha fell asleep on the couch and he left her there, heading to his bedroom to shower. He turned on the water, stripped and stepped beneath the spray, trying to wash away the dizzying fog of alcohol.

It was late. Too late. Owen probably would have been here by now if he were coming. Would have answered one of the three messages Jeremy had left for him when Tasha wasn't paying attention.

He's dealing with the problem. He'll have to come back eventually, if only to get his things. His roof isn't even fixed yet. He'll talk to you then.

His thoughts didn't comfort him. What if he didn't talk to him? Jeremy couldn't think of anything more painful than watching Owen Finn gathering his things, avoiding eye contact and conversation, and disappearing from his house and life, leaving an empty space that would never be filled.

He hoped Owen was okay. That his brothers weren't giving him too much grief. That it hadn't hurt him to see Tasha with Stephen. He hoped that somewhere, some part of Owen regretted that their time together had to end so soon.

You're being pathetic and needy. Stop embracing the damn cliché. It was what it was, nothing more.

And now it was over.

He turned off the shower and wandered into the bedroom while he was drying off. He could hardly look at the bed. When he did he saw Owen bending him over it after binding him in his suspenders. Owen waking up and smiling wickedly as soon as he saw him, ripping away the sheet to reveal his morning erection. Owen walking softly around the room as he dressed, not knowing Jeremy was awake.

He might have to get a new bed. He shook his head. Hell, if he started thinking like that, he'd end up burning the house down and moving to another state. Owen was everywhere. He always had been, even before they got together.

"Jeremy?" Tasha's call carried down the hallway.

"We've got company."

Owen? He wrapped his towel around his waist, wrenched open the door and forced himself not to run. Had Owen finally come back?

His heart cracked when he realized it was the wrong Finn.

"Jen?" He stopped and ran a hand through his wet hair in disbelief.

Did she know? Was she here to yell at him for taking advantage of her brother? For causing problems with her family?

Tasha's arms were around her and when Jen looked up, he could see tears in those eyes that reminded him so much of Owen's. "I need a place to stay for tonight, Jeremy. The wedding is off."

His first thought was, "Damn straight it's off." But he knew he couldn't say that out loud. She looked awful, poor thing. She'd come here for comfort? Oh hell.

He came toward them and wrapped his arms around both of them, hoping that his towel wouldn't slip. "I'm so sorry, Little Finn."

Tasha kissed her cheek. "Welcome to the Heartbreak Hotel, baby girl. Everyone who's been kicked in the ass by love is welcome here. Let's let Jeremy get dressed before he shocks your innocent eyes with his oversized sexiness and I'll pour you a shot of tequila."

He let her go, meeting Tasha's gaze with a question in his. She shrugged and shook her head, which meant neither of them knew why Jen had decided to come here of all places. He would call her parents, but honestly? He was too much of a damn coward. He needed to talk to Owen first. He needed to know what was going on.

Why the hell hadn't he called?

He got dressed as quickly as he could in his uniform of sweatpants and a t-shirt, his mind racing. Jen had been to his house a handful of times for barbecues by the lake with the rest of the Finn family, but she'd never come on her own.

The wedding was off, she'd said. That was his only clue.

Did she know what had happened? Did she know about Tasha and Jeremy's parts in it?

"Is this night ever going to end?" He sighed, heading back down the hallway to take care of the two women who were the most precious to him.

If he ever got his hands on Scott, Jeremy would be drawing his comics from prison.

CHAPTER ELEVEN

"Coffee. Thank God." He took a grateful sip and, not seeing the saint who'd brewed the pot, turned to his patio doors to enjoy the silence of the lake until the caffeine hit him enough that he could face this coming day.

He hadn't been able to sleep without Owen beside him. He could smell the man's scent on his pillows. Even when he'd ripped off the sheets and pillowcases and put on a freshly washed set, it was still there. Owen was still there.

But he hadn't called. All Jeremy had gotten was a one-line text he saw when he woke up this morning.

Will talk later.

It was a shitty way to wake up. The most unsatisfying

message in the history of texting. It gave him no clue where they stood, what Owen was thinking. Nothing. And later could mean an hour or a year. It felt like he was being blown off.

There were three women sitting on the balcony when he stepped outside, and they turned as soon as they heard him open the door.

Caught, Jeremy thought, like a deer in the damn headlights. "I'm sorry. I didn't mean to interrupt."

He started to go back inside but Owen's mother stopped him.

"Jeremy Porter, there you are, angel. We were wondering when we'd see your handsome face."

Angel. He was still an angel. She must not know.

"Mrs. Finn, good morning." He knew he looked shocked. He was. Shocked, barefoot and clinging to his coffee as if it were a life vest on a stormy sea as he looked down at Owen's perfectly put together mother. He lifted a hand to run it self-consciously through his tangled hair. "I didn't know you were here."

"We're family, you don't need to be formal." She smiled and gestured to the empty seat beside her. "And where else would I be when we have so much to talk about?"

Tasha bit her lip and stared down into her coffee cup. Jen's expression was apologetic, but more at peace than it had been last night.

Jeremy sat down abruptly. "Of course."

"I was just thanking Mama for taking care of everything," Jen offered helpfully. "Cancellations and gift returns. She's been checking things off the list since dawn."

"It's the least I can do," Mrs. Finn insisted, her shock of short, red curls bouncing as she nodded. "I should have kicked that boy out of the house when you first started dating him. I'm sorry dear, but you know I'm right. He was never good enough for you."

"Everybody knew," Jen responded glumly. "I didn't listen."

Jeremy kept his head down. This was getting surreal. First Tasha, then Jen and now Ellen Finn. He was being invaded. Were they forming a kindly mob to politely run him out of town? Kill him with kindness?

Why was she here?

He'd found out last night that Seamus had been the one to sit Jen down and tell her about everything. Her fiancé's stealing. His flirting. His threats to the Finn brothers and the images he'd sent. He'd thought she deserved to know. To be a part of the family meeting, since it directly related to her fiancé.

She'd handled it well. She'd shown Jeremy a snapshot of herself holding an embarrassing if not incriminating picture of Scott in one hand and a burning wedding invitation in the other. She was saving it to send to him after her brothers made sure he couldn't use the ones *he'd* sent against them.

Jennifer was a Finn through and through.

And her kindness didn't surprise him either. She didn't make any judgments about Stephen and Tasha or Owen and Jeremy. No, like the rest of them, her recriminations were entirely self-directed. She knew. She should have known. Her stubborn ignorance had brought this on her family.

It had taken more than few shots of tequila and a whole lot of talking to set her straight.

Jeremy glanced at Ellen Finn from beneath his lashes. They were all out of tequila now. How much did she know?

And where the hell was Owen?

Will talk later.

"Jeremy? Jen told me how much you helped her last night. And she also shared your thoughts on the Finns."

His Finn Factor speech? Jeremy grimaced at Jen. What had he said exactly? "I hate to admit this, Mrs. Finn, but I'm pretty sure I was three sheets to the wind at the time. I didn't mean to offend anyone."

Ellen reached out and patted his arm. "I've always liked you, Jeremy. Maybe it's because you're an artist and a people watcher like me. And you saw something I didn't...in more than one of my children. A mother's love can sometimes blind her to what's right in front of her. I'm very proud of my family's success, but I don't think I tell them enough that I'll be proud of anything they choose, anyone they choose, as long as it makes them happy."

She couldn't be saying what he thought she was. Then again, this was Ellen Finn. His throat tightened and he leaned forward earnestly. "Mrs. Finn, you are the best mother I know who wasn't written for television. Your kids, *all* your kids, know they're loved."

"We do, Mama." Jen wiped a tear from her eye quickly, but not before her mother noticed and seemed to get a little weepy herself.

"Your father and I have never been more proud of you, darling. It takes a brave woman to acknowledge her mistakes and pick herself back up again." Ellen looked at Jeremy then. "And I hope *you* know Shawn and I think of you as another son, Jeremy. We've always been proud of you too."

Jeremy started to thank her, but almost spilled his coffee down his t-shirt when a familiar male voice came from the side of the house, beneath the balcony. "Are you talking about me, woman?"

"Yes, dear," Ellen called down, standing as he came up the stairs. "We didn't hear you knock but, oh good, you brought breakfast fixings. These three look like they could use something more than coffee." She turned to a beet-red Jeremy. "Do you mind if I take over your kitchen for a bit?"

Dear God, this had to be a dream. A weird, slightly terrifying but beautiful dream brought on by the evil tequila. "Please. Can I help you with anything?"

Shawn Finn stopped by his chair and held out his hand. "Good man to offer, but that's my job. Think of it as my way of apologizing for the female invasion you've had to endure all morning."

Standing automatically, Jeremy looked down in surprise at the outstretched hand, then took it and smiled at the broad-shouldered older man, whose blond hair was still thick but liberally streaked with gray. "Thank you, sir, but it's been a pleasure."

"Smart boy."

The couple disappeared into his house and he walked over to stand in front of Tasha and Jen, lowering his voice. "Am I awake? Did I eat the worm? What's happening?"

"I don't know," Tasha groaned. "But it's freaking me out."

Jen snorted. "How many years have you known us? You know what we Finns do whenever trouble crops up."

They closed ranks and banded together. "Yes, but you don't usually do it in my house."

She reached up and patted his hip, smiling at the frowning Tasha. "You're both a part of this family. My parents know it even if you don't. So suck it up, guys, and feel the love. I don't know about you, but I'm starving."

When she left, Jeremy held out his hand to Tasha. "Join me at the dock for coffee and crying?"

"Please." She pulled him down the stairs, her coffee still clutched in one hand. "You need a boat."

"It's a lake, Tasha. You can circle a lake, but you can't make a clean getaway if that's what you're thinking. We're stuck."

"He's right," said Stephen, who was leaning against a wooden post at the bottom of the stairs. "For a clean getaway you'd need a plane."

No longer surprised by magically appearing Finns this morning, Jeremy nodded in his direction. "I'll get on that right after the homeowner's association installs my runway."

Stephen Finn looked the way Jeremy felt. His light brown hair was mussed, there were shadows under his blue eyes and his tie was loose and limp around his neck. It was obvious he hadn't gone to bed. "Hey, Jeremy. Natasha."

Tasha turned toward him, clinging to Jeremy's hand. "Good morning, Senator. There's coffee upstairs. You look like you could use it."

"Thanks, but I need to talk to you first." He glanced apologetically at Jeremy. "Alone, if that's okay with you."

Jeremy nodded, releasing Tasha and taking a step back. "Should I be expecting the entire family?" he asked carefully.

Stephen put his hand on Tasha's shoulder as soon as she reached his side, as if he needed to assure himself she wasn't going anywhere. "Seamus is getting his neighbor to watch the kids then he'll be by."

He hesitated, studying Jeremy with an inscrutable expression. "Owen had something he insisted he had to do. He wasn't sure he would make it for breakfast."

"Oh." The message couldn't be any clearer—the trouble might be over, but Owen was done with him.

A sharp knife couldn't have cut more deeply.

Taking a shaky breath, Jeremy nodded. "I'll leave you two alone then."

"Jeremy wait." Stephen sighed, rubbing the stubble on his jaw. "You should know… It's been dealt with. Our problem. Lucky for us, Scott is a moron. Man didn't even make copies. And what we had on him sealed the deal."

"Good," was all Jeremy could manage. He needed to get away from the Finns. He didn't want them to see him like this.

"He's not coming? I'm going to kill him," Tasha exclaimed to Stephen as he set off down the shoreline.

Though he was genuinely appreciative of her outrage on his behalf, Jeremy kept walking, uncertain he could keep the pain from spilling out. The family descending on his house en mass was a gesture that almost moved him to tears. They knew, or most of them did, and they were still here.

They were still here.

How much of that was for Jen and how much of it was for him he wasn't sure, but none of them had treated him with disrespect or disgust. Owen's father had shaken his hand, for God's sake. His mother had told him she was proud of him.

Owen was the Finn who was a no-show. His lover. His best friend. Owen was the one rejecting what they had. What they could have. Not his family. Him.

Will talk later.

He sat down on the dock and stared at the ripples the wind made on the water. Sunlight skimmed the surface and made it sparkle like diamonds, but the sight didn't bring him the peace it usually did.

His heart had whiplash. As quickly and abruptly as their fling had started, it was over. He'd always known it would end, though, hadn't he? Always known it was temporary.

The other shoe had finally fallen hard and all he could think about now was yesterday morning.

He should have woken Owen with the kind of kiss he loved. Should have taken him in his mouth and made him moan in pleasure. He should have touched him more and thanked him properly for breakfast. For making him realize that he wanted more. He wanted the kind of family and laughter and love that was currently taking over his house. He wanted someone to share his life with, and yes, he wanted a dog. Maybe even a child. Someday. Because he had a lot of love to give.

The problem was he couldn't imagine doing that with anyone but Owen.

He wasn't sure how long he sat there, lost in his personal suffering, but footsteps on the dock made him look up distractedly. He forced a smile. "Seamus. You made it."

Stephen's twin sat down beside him, knees bent and arms wrapped around his legs. His hair was a little longer and wavier than Stephen's precision cut, and he wore a faded flannel over a washed out t-shirt instead of a suit and tie. Other than that and the scar that curved roguishly on Stephen's chin, the two were identical.

Their personalities, however, were polar opposites.

"Mom has a plate waiting for you in the kitchen. She's putting on a good show, but I can tell she's starting to get a little worried. Are you ever planning on coming in again? It is your house."

Jeremy shook his head. "I'm sorry. I'm being rude, I know. I just needed a minute."

"You're being human," Seamus told him. "It's allowed, considering the bombshell that just dropped on all of us. My vote was for maiming, in case you were wondering. Torture and maiming. Sadly, Stephen shot me down. Apparently his constituents frown on that sort of thing."

"I would've backed you up," Jeremy said grimly. "I still will. It's not too late."

"It's done. He knows better than to come near us again, and we all had a cathartic laugh when Jen sent him that picture. And then posted it on Instagram. She earned that, but now it's time to move forward. If I were talking to my kids, I'd tell them there's a lesson in this. More than one."

"Oh yeah?" What? Always listen to your first instincts? Don't sleep with men who aren't gay? Never kiss in public because all phones have cameras?

"Secrets rarely stay secret for long, so you may as well be honest from the start," Seamus said. "And love is a blessing, no matter what form it takes."

Jeremy looked at him and sighed. "Wise words. No wonder women keep leaving children on your doorstep."

Seamus chuckled at the familiar line. "Father of the year, that's me. I had a good teacher."

"I didn't."

Seamus studied him. "No, you didn't. But you're still one of the better men I know. And if you're as smart as we all know you are, you won't give in to defeat and despair so easily. I don't think things are as dark as they might seem."

With Owen? "I think you might be wrong about that one."

"Both my brothers are good men, Jeremy. Good talkers as a rule, except when it comes to their feelings. It doesn't mean they don't have them."

Did he think there was still a chance? And was Seamus Finn giving Jeremy his approval to date his previously straight brother?

Seamus suddenly smiled. "You brood too much. Don't go Van Gogh on us, Porter. You draw comics, not sunflowers. Just come and have breakfast and smile at my mother so she knows she can leave."

Feeling better but still afraid to hope, Jeremy stood. "Yes, sir."

As they walked slowly back toward his house, Seamus glanced at him curiously. "Speaking of secrets, did you know about Stephen and Natasha?"

"Never had a clue." And he should have.

Seamus whistled. "That is a long damn time to keep something like that from us. Kind of blows my advice all to hell, doesn't it?"

"You didn't know either?"

Shaking his head, Seamus said, "Just because we're twins doesn't mean we're connected at the hip, and we must have been standing in the other line when they were handing out psychic bonds. Stephen plays things pretty close to the vest—the stronger he feels, the less you know." He shrugged. "I'm more upset with myself to be honest. Apparently, I'm the only Finn brother not doing something exciting or scandalous enough to lie about. How sad is that?"

Jeremy's smile was rueful. "There's always tomorrow."

"Tomorrow I'll still have four kids, a family business and a life full of to-do lists. Doesn't exactly leave a lot of time for bad behavior."

"You're a Finn. You'll find a way."

And Jeremy would have a lot of free time on his hands now that needed to be filled. Maybe he could babysit.

CHAPTER TWELVE

The sound of a crash from another room woke Jeremy from a restless sleep. Everyone had gone home hours ago, so he jolted out of bed, instantly alert. If someone had picked tonight of all nights to break into his damn house, whoever it was would be sorry. He was eager to hit something. Someone. All he needed was the right excuse.

He walked silently down the dark hall, listening.

Somebody was in his office. Swearing.

Recognizing the voice, Jeremy ground his teeth together. He leaned on the doorjamb and flipped the wall switch, blinking against the bright light that flooded the room. A familiar figure knelt on the floor beside his drafting table, trying to pick up the shards of what used to be a porcelain collectible of one of his comic book characters.

"You broke my demon."

Owen looked up and winced. "Hell, I'm sorry. I'm not as light on my feet as I used to be."

Jeremy looked at the open window and shook his head. "You climbed in through my window?"

"You bolted the door." Owen stood and placed the shards on the table, brushing off his hands. "It's the strangest thing. My key doesn't work when you bolt the door. But since I know you always forget to lock this window I... Yeah. I guess I should have knocked."

"Yes." Jeremy wanted to be glad to see him, but it hurt too much. "You missed your family. All of them. Tasha too."

Suddenly thirsty, he turned and headed for the kitchen.

Owen followed. "I know I did. There were a few things I had to do first and I figured you'd have so much company you wouldn't notice. Then the day got away from me. I heard Jen spent the night, though. Thank you for that. I think she needed to step away from everything for a while."

Jeremy got a glass from the cupboard and filled it

with water, taking a deep, much-needed drink before he spoke again. "Why are you here, Finn? It's late."

Owen's expression changed from apology to surprise, then it hardened. "What do you mean, why am I here? I'm staying here. I have a key, remember?"

"Don't play this game, Owen. If you wanted to slip in while I was asleep to grab your things, I get that. I won't stop you."

"You won't stop me?" Owen crossed his arms, his biceps straining against the short sleeves of his white shirt. "Then you're a better man than I am, Porter. If our roles were reversed and you tried to sneak away like an adolescent tool, I'd tie you up and punish you until you apologized and begged to stay."

He's defensive, that's all. He doesn't want to look like the bad guy.

Jeremy tried to slow his racing heart. "I'm fine, Owen, and according to your brother, the problem is solved. We're good. No explanations necessary. Do you want me to help you with your bags? I put them in the guest room."

"You packed my bags?" Owen turned away, anger in every stride as he headed down the hall, glancing back to make sure Jeremy followed him. "So now what? I walk away in the dark of night and we forget about the last two weeks? I'll meet you for darts at the pub and you can tell me about the new man you're breaking in with Tasha? Unless she's busy with my brother, that is. Is that the plan?"

Jeremy was unable to remain silent. "Are you drunk or just cruel? You're the one who didn't come back last night, who didn't answer my calls when you had to know I was worried as hell about what was going on."

"I sent you a text."

"*Will talk later*," Jeremy sneered. "Yeah, I got that ode to man-speak. I also noticed that you were the only member of your family who didn't come over today. The *only* one, and I don't have to be a genius to get that message. So don't stand there and blame me so you can feel better about yourself for ending your curiosity experiment."

Owen dropped the bags he'd just picked up and pushed Jeremy against the wall. "Are you *trying* to piss me off?"

"Gonna hit me? Go ahead, Master Finn," Jeremy fired back. "You couldn't hurt me any more than you already have."

Light blue eyes clouded in confusion and worry as

they studied his face. Jeremy didn't look away or struggle. *Let him see what he's done*, he thought wearily. What did it matter now?

Even in this, he was weak. He never thought he'd be this close to Owen again.

When the hands gripping his shirt unclenched and started to touch him, he let out a shaky breath. Owen's hands were on his chest. His shoulders. Cupping his neck.

"Hurt you?" Owen repeated softly. "That's the last thing I mean to do. I thought you knew..." He slipped his hand under Jeremy's shirt and pressed it against his hard stomach. "Here. It didn't need to be said. You've always known, Jeremy. Haven't you?"

Owen kissed him and Jeremy tried to turn his head away but the stubborn man followed, thrusting his tongue inside and taking what he wanted. Jeremy shivered, melting against the wall. Damn him. Did he want to take everything with him when he left, including his pride?

Jeremy moaned when Owen's hand slid into his sweatpants and gripped his hardening erection.

No. If he's leaving he needs to go. It feels good now, but you'll hate yourself when it's over.

"Owen, stop. Yellow, damn it."

The hand on him disappeared and Owen stepped back, surprising him. He turned away and punched the wall so hard it left a dent. "Mother fucking—"

"Jesus, Owen. Did you break something?"

"No doubt," Owen laughed raggedly, leaning against the damage. "I fell in through your window and landed on my bad knee, broke your demon into slivers that I'll be finding for weeks and punched your very solid wall like an idiot. But that's not what really hurts." He looked into Jeremy's eyes. "You mean it. You really want me to go, and it's my fault. I made a decision and just acted without thinking again. Without talking. I gave you this smooth speech about communication and honesty when I wanted to paddle your ass, but when it comes to us—to you and me—I keep getting it wrong."

The pained frustration in his voice got to Jeremy. They had too much between them for it to end like this. "Getting what wrong, Owen? Talk to me. We're still friends, right?"

Owen shook his head, rubbing his sore knuckles. "No, I can't. Not until I show you something. Come with me."

Jeremy hesitated before following him toward the

front door. "Can it wait? We should get some ice on that hand."

"Come to the door, Jeremy."

Owen unlocked the front door and waited for him, looking defeated. "You know I actually thought it would be a good idea, having the family come over for breakfast without me. 'He'll see that everything's really okay,' I thought. 'That they aren't pretending to accept him, us, for my sake.' Of course, my brilliant plan neglected to take into account the fact that nobody else knew about it."

He sighed and pushed open the door. "Then I got a flat tire. 'I can't call now,' I thought. 'I'll ruin the big surprise.' Once again, I didn't think about how long it would take me to change a tire by myself in the dark, or that you'd come to the conclusion that I wasn't coming back. That I would do that to you. It never crossed my mind, so why would it ever cross yours?" He pointed toward the driveway. "Look, damn it. Underneath the streetlight."

Jeremy stepped onto the front porch and stared. Then he blinked. It was still there. A *U-Haul* trailer was attached to Owen's truck. A moving trailer? It couldn't mean what he thought it did. Could it?

Licking his dry lips, trying to curtail the swelling of hope in his chest, he asked, "So...is that apartment roof too expensive to fix?"

"It's not my problem since I don't live there anymore. I handed the landlord my keys this afternoon. Sucker kept my deposit too. I'm officially homeless."

Jeremy turned toward Owen, a million questions in his mind, but all he could ask was, "Why?"

Owen reached out and pulled him back inside, closing and locking the door before leaning against it. "Why didn't I call you last night? I'll admit the first meeting of the brothers after that text was rough. Mostly because we don't keep secrets, as a rule. At least, I thought we didn't. Stephen should have told us about Natasha years ago, and I—well, they were as surprised as you might imagine about you and me." He sighed. "By the time all the confusion died down, it was so late I didn't know whether I was coming or going, and I fell asleep on the floor in the family room while listening to Stephen make deals and plot villainous deeds on the phone."

"You should have called."

Owen nodded. "I should have called. But let's address the question of the trailer. Am I right in thinking that you want to know why I brought my lucky, ugly lounge chair, my shamrock lamp and the rest of my things over to your house when we've never actually discussed the prospect of living together?"

"I would like to know that, yes."

He smiled tiredly and Jeremy felt the hope swell out of control, filling his heart painfully.

"You know how I am when I get an idea in my head, Porter," Owen told him. "I had this crazy notion that we could live together. That I could stay with you. Be with you and only you. I wasn't ready for these two weeks to end and I... well, I knew I never would be. I didn't want to give you the chance to overthink it and say no before I could convince you it was a good idea."

Be with you and only you.

Fighting for breath, for calm, Jeremy ran both hands through his hair. "This isn't a temporary agreement you're talking about, is it? What you're talking about is living together. Other people are bound to find out. People you work with. You're talking about a relationship. With me, after only a few weeks. With me, your male friend from high school who remembers how excited you were for months after Janet Leary let you touch her—"

"*Yes,*" Owen interrupted, raising his voice in frustration. "I admit it, I love the female body. I respect and adore the goddess within. I've worshipped blissfully at the altar of the pussy for decades."

Jeremy covered his mouth to hide his unexpected smile. "I know that altar."

"I'm aware, and if Natasha hadn't been secretly rocking my brother's world, I might have convinced you to let her join us on holidays and special occasions. Hell, maybe for our tenth anniversary we can talk about it, or something like it."

"Wait…" Jeremy blinked at him. "Our tenth anniversary?"

Owen sighed again. "Damn it, Jeremy, what is it I have to say to get through to you? You know what you mean to me. You've always been the first one I want to tell my news to, good and bad. You've always been the most important person in my life who wasn't related to me by blood. But…well, I've been thinking about you differently for a while now, since your date with what's-her-name—"

"Darla?"

He nodded. "Since Darla. Don't ask me why, but after that I went through a lot of women trying to get the idea of being with you out of my mind. Then the party at Tasha's happened and you looked at me for that split second and I thought there was a chance you thought about me too. And after that first night? The last few weeks? What you make me feel... I've never felt like that before. Like I can be myself and more than myself at the same time. I spend my day watching the clock because I can't wait to come home to you. Just to be *home* with you. I wake up earlier than I have to so I can watch you fucking sleep, and I'm not stupid enough to let something that good get away. Bisexual, kinky, gay, straight—I don't give a flying fuck what you or anyone else wants to call it. You're my best friend and I happen to be in love with you. Does the rest of it really matter?"

He'd said it. The only words Jeremy had ever needed to hear.

"Nothing else matters," he assured him, joining him in three long strides and pulling him into his arms for a blistering kiss.

Then he lifted his head with a breathless laugh, relief fizzing through him, making him feel lighter than air. Jesus, he'd thought it was over. He hadn't known, hadn't had any idea that Owen would ever love him back. That he was even thinking in terms of forever.

"You suck at communicating outside of the bedroom, you know that?" he complained.

Owen was staring at his lips. "I'll do better. You'll teach me. Until then, let's go communicate where I'm at my best."

"What about your hand?"

"Forget it. I need you now."

"You've got me." He took Owen's good hand and led him to the bedroom, joy and lust and love battling for dominance inside him. Owen was here, where he belonged. And he wasn't going anywhere.

He loves me.

Jeremy went to the dresser and pulled out his suspenders, and Owen paused at his belt after taking off his shirt. "Those uncomfortable things better be for you."

He shook his head, stalking his prey. "Over twenty-four hours of torture, Owen. Of loving you and wondering if I was losing my only family, my best friend and my lover in one fell swoop. Twenty-four hours of forcing myself to breathe and eat and talk to people when I just wanted to stop the world until you came back to me."

"*Loving* me?"

Jeremy nodded. "Completely and, until ten minutes ago, hopelessly. I've loved you for a long time. I never thought I could have you, and not just because you didn't like men. Your family is my family. *You* are my family, Owen. If I lost you..." His voice broke. "All I want to do now is tie you to my headboard, kiss every inch of you and make love to you with the cock you say you can't get enough of. Nothing else, I promise. I just need you not to distract me."

Owen's cheeks were flushed. "For you, Jeremy. Only for you. But just one time."

We'll see.

He watched Owen finish undressing, studying the body he couldn't get enough of. No agreements, no rules, no limits or labels, just Owen. It sounded too good to be true, but here he was, naked and kneeling on Jeremy's bed. "Where do you want me?"

"Everywhere," Jeremy groaned. "But for now lie on your back and put your hands over your head."

"On my back?" Owen hesitated but then obeyed, his expression expectant. Aroused.

Jeremy tore off his shirt and pushed down his sweatpants before climbing onto the bed beside his lover. He leaned over him, suspenders in hand. "Grip the headboard."

"Don't make it too tight."

"Yes, Master Finn."

Owen breathed out a laugh. "Don't think I'm going to forget this when it's my turn."

Jeremy bent down and kissed him softly on the lips. "I promise I'll make sure you won't."

Owen's eyes darkened to a stormy blue as Jeremy wrapped the suspenders around his wrist and the headboard, tying a knot that was sloppy but effective. "Too tight?"

Owen shook his head.

"Good. Now let me welcome you home properly."

Jeremy kissed and touched every inch of Owen he could reach, taking his time until he was squirming and swearing softly beneath him.

"Jeremy, damn it."

"What is it, Owen? Don't you like it?"

"I love it," he growled. "But you know what I need."

"Oh I do. You always need it. I love how greedy you get. How bossy. Order me to do it. Tell me what you want."

Owen spoke through gritted teeth. "I want you to suck my cock."

Jeremy took a steadying breath, moving until he was between Owen's spread thighs, and then reached for the bedside bottle of lube. "Yes, Master Finn."

He poured some lube onto his fingers then lowered himself until his own aching erection was pressed against the bed and his wet fingers were sliding between Owen's ass cheeks. "Have I told you how hard I get when you make me get on my knees to suck you off? That I think about it every day? Think about coming to your office at lunch? You're right. I would do it anywhere. Anytime, just to feel you lose control, grip my hair until my scalp stings and fuck my mouth with your delicious cock. "

"Jesus, Jeremy."

He pushed one finger deep in Owen's ass and heard him moan. "Do you like the way I communicate? I'm learning from the best. Maybe I should tell you how much I loved having you deep inside me. Only you, Owen. No one else has ever made me want to beg for it. You can bend me over your desk, the bed, anywhere you want and take me as hard and fast as you need to and I will never say no. But right now I want this more."

"Oh, you're a teasing bastard." Owen's growl turned into a moan of pleasure when Jeremy's mouth opened over his erection.

He took him deep while his finger started thrusting in and out of his ass.

"*Yes.* Fuck yeah, Jeremy." Owen's hips lifted helplessly, his knees bending and heels digging into the mattress. "It's so good, babe. God, you know I love it."

He knew. Jeremy savored the salt of him, tracing each vein and ridge with his tongue and swallowing until he felt the pearly drop on the head of Owen's shaft and knew he was close.

Love you, baby. Gonna make you come so hard.

He pressed his finger against Owen's prostate and rubbed, sucking harder when he heard Owen shout his name. "Jeremy!"

His eyes closed as Owen came, the hot taste filling his mouth and going to his head like an aphrodisiac. Now he would take him like this. Face to face. Nothing between them.

He rose onto his knees and reached for the lube again, coating his erection as he watched Owen shudder with aftershocks. Bracing one hand on the bed, he came down over Owen's body and used the other hand to grip the base of his shaft. "Look at me."

Beautiful blue eyes dilated with passion met his.

"Welcome home, Owen Finn."

When the head of his cock pressed through the ring of tight muscles that led to heaven, Jeremy let out a ragged groan. "*Oh, baby.*"

"Fuck," Owen gasped out, wrapping his legs around Jeremy's waist. "Untie me. I want to touch you."

"Fuck off," Jeremy growled playfully. His hips slung forward, slowly filling the ass that was so tight around him it made him see stars. "This is mine. All mine."

Owen's legs tightened, pulling him closer. Deeper. "Jesus, that is a big, fat cock. I need it all, Jeremy. Fuck me."

Jeremy leaned down and brushed his lips across Owen's, pressing their foreheads together. "Love you," he corrected softly, determined not to let Owen drive him to rush this. "I'm loving you, Owen. Let me."

An expression of vulnerability crossed Owen's face. "Love me then. Just…don't stop."

Surprised and breathless with love, Jeremy vowed, "Never."

He kissed Owen again as he started to move, pumping slow and deep inside his lover. His.

You're mine, Owen. Truly mine.

So good, he thought, his tongue dueling with Owen's

and his hips rocking gently against him. *So good, baby.*

Owen tore his mouth away with a groan. "You're trying to kill me as punishment. I swear I'll call next time. You can even grow that damn beard back if you want to. Just—I need it."

"What do you need, baby?"

Owen snarled, clamping his thighs on Jeremy's waist almost painfully. "Love me *harder*."

Jeremy shuddered, unable to resist the demand. "Yes, Master Finn."

"I'll show you Master Finn. As soon as I get free I'm going to spank that ass so—*Jesus*, yes. *Fuck.* Jeremy, *yes!*"

Jeremy was powering into him, deep and hard the way he knew Owen needed it. The way *he* needed it. He looked into those blue eyes and watched Owen's face transform as sensation overwhelmed him. "You love it. Love me. You can't get enough."

Owen's head was pressing back hard on the pillow beneath him. "I'll never get enough. Christ, like that. Don't stop. Don't stop, Jeremy. I love it. Love you. God knows I do."

Jeremy felt the red haze of need pull him under as he started to lose control. He was so close. He never wanted to stop but he was so damn close... "Owen!"

He pumped his hips as the scalding jets of his climax filled the ass beneath him. Owen was muttering his name and moaning for him but all Jeremy could do was let the waves wash over him, his body shuddering. "So good."

It took a few minutes to recover, but then he kissed Owen again, pulling out gently and rolling off the bed to grab a wet washcloth from the bathroom. He came back and slid the cloth over his lover's body tenderly. "Your turn for aftercare. Damn, you are a perfect specimen, Owen Finn. I want to draw you like this."

Owen chuckled. "Well it's not an explosion, but you'd probably sell more copies because, yes, I *am* that attractive."

He used the cloth to snap him on his hip and Owen yelped and then scowled. "What did you want me to say? Do it, Jeremy? Draw me like one of your French gi—"

When Jeremy covered his mouth with a hand, Owen's eyes sparkled with laughter.

He couldn't help but smile in return. "And now the moment is ruined." Owen licked his palm and Jeremy lifted his hand with a sigh. "What?"

"If you untie me, I'll go make us some breakfast to

celebrate our first successful round of make-up sex."

He reached up to untangle the knot of his suspenders. "The first round?"

Owen nodded. "I know neither of us has actually been in a relationship before, but I've heard from people who have that make-up sex is vital. I also think it doesn't count as an actual cessation of hostilities unless you do it three times."

"You're just making things up now." He released Owen's wrists and rubbed his arms gently. "How do you feel? How's your hand?"

Owen grimaced. "I think I could use that ice."

Jeremy leaned over to kiss his knuckles. "How about we get ice on that and *I* make breakfast?"

Owen slid off the bed and into Jeremy's arms. "You like taking care of me, don't you? See how nice it is when you let someone stick around?"

"I see." Jeremy nodded. "I'm glad you don't take no for an answer."

Owen smiled, looking pleased. "Is it too late for naked Xbox?"

Jeremy sighed and shook his head. Some things hadn't changed. "Sports or swords?"

He felt a hand grip his stirring erection and shivered.

"Swords," Owen declared with a challenging grin. "And to the victor goes the paddle."

Jeremy smiled back at him, wondering how quickly he could throw the game.

Welcome home, Owen Finn.

CHAPTER THIRTEEN

"Where is he anyway?"

Jeremy looked up from his drawing. Jennifer Finn was at the end of the dock, supposedly attempting to fish. In reality, she was posing as if she were attempting to fish, but it served his purpose.

"Your brother?" he asked. "I don't know. He was just going to the grocery store. He should have been back by now."

He glanced over his shoulder and saw Shawn and Ellen Finn on the balcony, talking softly to each other while they enjoyed the day. They'd become frequent visitors at his house lately, and Jeremy couldn't be happier. It felt more like a home now.

"I'm glad he isn't back yet. I've been working up the

nerve to talk to you about something."

That sounded ominous. Jeremy set down his sketchbook and stood, walking over to sit down beside her. "Okay, I'm ready," he said, letting his legs dangle over the edge. "Lay it on me."

"So, you and Owen have been together now for a few months," she started.

Three. Three months and five days. "Yes, we have."

"Are you happy?"

"Blissfully."

"Things have changed a lot, for both of you I know. But for Owen, well, Tasha told me he was always at the club before, but he's only gone back twice since you two have been a thing." She paused. "She also told me both times you went with him."

Jeremy could feel his face heating. They'd agreed to go once a month and let Jeremy see what it was like. To meet some of Owen's friends in the lifestyle. They'd been so friendly and welcoming, so accepting of Owen's same-sex relationship, that it made Jeremy want to go back. It really was like its own little community of tolerance. With leather and paddles.

But he wasn't telling Jennifer *any* of that. "Do you just sit around all day thinking up uncomfortable conversations to have with me when we're alone? Is Tasha coaching you?"

Jen laughed, pushing a stray strawberry blonde hair back into the wide-brimmed hat he'd convinced her to wear for his sketch. He'd finished his current deadline and decided to try his hand at a different style just for fun. He was enjoying the challenge.

She shook her head. "No, Jeremy, I swear. It's just, I've decided I'm ready to go ahead and make a date with…someone from the club. I told you about it before, right—the negotiations?"

"Oh yes, I remember," Jeremy said wryly. "Tasha's friend."

"Do you like it?" Jennifer's voice was subdued and hesitant. "I mean it's still pretty new to you, right? The kinky stuff? But blissfully happy has to mean you like it."

Jeremy sighed, rubbing the back of his neck as he considered his response. "It depends on who you're with, Jen. I think it should be someone who really knows what they're doing. Someone you feel like you can trust with your physical safety. If Tasha suggested him, I trust that. She's a hellion, but she wouldn't steer you wrong. Have you met him?"

Jen blushed and looked down at the fishing pole in her hands. "A few times for coffee. And we've talked on the phone. He's sexier than I was expecting."

Jeremy narrowed his eyes. "Be careful, Jennifer. I mean, from what I understand, even with partners who aren't in a relationship, things can get intense fairly quickly. You don't want to mistake that for more than it is."

The youngest Finn made a face. "Believe me, I'm not looking for a boyfriend. I've only been single for two months of my adult life, and I plan on enjoying myself. But this guy, well you're right. Very intense. The closer we get to our play date, the more dangerous it seems. He's even mentioned bringing in someone else if I'd like." She bit her lip. "It's actually pretty damn exciting."

He groaned. "Why are you telling me this? Stop telling me things like this."

She laughed, but Jeremy shook his head. "I'm not kidding. A very intense, dangerous guy from a fetish club is taking Little Finn out for whips and chains with a possible side of three-ways. What am I supposed to do with that information?"

"You keep it a secret. You always do."

"And I always will," he sighed. "Though your brother Seamus had some very wise words about secrets that I would share with you…if I could remember them. The gist is they're bad, and you shouldn't have any."

Jen smiled. "That's a man rule. Men aren't allowed to have secrets. They don't know what to do with them. But every girl gets to keep a few. It's one of the perks. I just happen to keep them with you. And Tasha of course. She's going to be there in case I need to make a getaway."

"Thank God," Jeremy said, relieved. "Just tell her to tell me when I need to make sure your brother stays home. And be safe, Jen. I mean, have fun, have adventures, go crazy because you deserve it after all that insanity…but be safe."

She leaned against him affectionately and he wrapped his arm around her shoulder. She was a Finn. She would do whatever the hell she wanted.

And he would always be here to keep her secrets and kick the ass of anyone who hurt her.

He heard Owen shouting for him. "Jeremy? Damn it, a little help over here, please!"

"Duty calls." He jumped up and went running toward the house, seeing Owen struggling with something in his arms at the foot of the stairs.

Something wriggling excitedly.

"You didn't."

He smiled at Jeremy and then grunted when a paw whacked him in the stomach. "Sadly, I did."

Jennifer's squeal of delight increased the animal's excitement. "A puppy? You brought home a *puppy*?"

"Oh, it's so cute," Ellen Finn called down from the patio. "Shawn, did you see? Owen got them a dog."

Owen handed the bundle of red and amber fur to Jeremy. "I did. Consider him a bonus birthday present."

Jeremy laughed when the tiny black-nosed imp licked his face. "A baby boy. Hello, boy. What do we name him?"

Owen's hand came up to scratch the dog behind his ears, as if he couldn't help himself. "I don't know. I suppose we could name him after my favorite thing."

Jeremy grinned at him and Owen scowled as his ears turned red. Guess they weren't naming him after *that* favorite thing.

Jen jumped in. "Pizza?"

"You're both smartasses," Owen grumbled. "What about Xbox? Or Boogie?"

"Boogie?" she frowned.

Jeremy glared in warning at Owen, who was trying to embarrass him as payback. "Let's try something less obscure. He's a stubborn one—look at how determined he is to get down and play. He's a Finn."

"I had a dog named Angus when I was a boy," Shawn Finn said as he walked down the steps to inspect the newest member of the family. "Damn thing bit my leg three times and ate all my mother's good cushions, but it's a good name."

Ellen joined him, squinting at her phone. "Wait, I need to take a picture, and then Jen can use my phone to find a baby name site. We'll pick the perfect one. Stand closer to Jeremy, Owen. Oh, you three look adorable."

"Badass," Owen crossed his arms, nodding in finality beside him. "His name is Badass Finn."

Jeremy smiled for the picture, then looked down at the angelic puppy face and shook his head. "Don't worry. We'll find you a name you can be proud of. One we can shout in public when you inevitably escape your leash. Until then, welcome to the family, Badass."

***

Owen was in the living room playing with the puppy and setting up his sleeping crate when Jeremy joined him, handing him a beer. "How's our little Badass?"

"He's earned his name already," Owen answered, watching the tiny bundle tug on the rope toy in his hand. "He's got a lot of energy too. I was thinking of slipping some beer into his food dish to knock him out."

"Don't you dare." Jeremy sat down on the floor beside him.

"Hey, what were you and Jen whispering about before they left?"

Shit. "Nothing important. She's still dealing with wedding backlash, I think. Antsy to get out into the world and find her place."

"Well, I wish Seamus hadn't let her move into the cottage behind the pub. That's no place for a young, single girl on her own. Maybe she needs a guard dog like Badass. He did have a few brothers and sisters who hadn't found a home."

"She'll be fine, Owen. She has us to look out for her." He patted the ground and laughed when the puppy pounced on his hand. "I can't believe you did this. I thought we'd decided to wait a while before we made the shared pet kind of commitment."

Owen slid his fingers into the hair at the base of Jeremy's neck and pulled him closer for a kiss. Oh, that tug. He loved it when he did that. It made him shiver. "It doesn't get more committed than this, babe. You know that. And he was begging to come home with me. With us."

Jeremy's throat tightened. "Thank you."

"You're welcome." Owen grinned. "So far, I have to say I think I'm pretty good at this relationship business."

"Cocky bastard." But Jeremy didn't disagree.

Every day, Owen surprised him. This was new to both of them, committing to a long-term monogamous relationship, but it came so naturally now. It was as if they'd both been waiting, storing up all the love they had to give until they found the right person to give it to.

And the sex. He couldn't forget about that. For two men who'd been known to like variety in their sexual partners, neither one of them was complaining. It kept getting better. Jeremy's trust with Owen's control. Owen's love of his more primal urges... He couldn't imagine ever being tempted to stray. And if he still had any doubts about Owen changing his mind about him— well, they were fast disappearing.

His Finn had taken on the task of communicating his feelings with the same gusto and stubborn determination he did with everything else. And once those floodgates had opened, Jeremy couldn't help but be sure of his heart. Owen loved him. Only him. He told him every day in word and deed. And it was better and stronger than any dream he'd ever had.

Everyone in the family could see how good they were together and for each other. They'd embraced him the same way they always had. Most importantly, they both felt it. This was right. This was the real thing.

Badass barked impatiently to get their attention.

"I think someone needs a walk before bed." Jeremy stood up, holding his hand out for Owen.

"*I* think someone should hurry up and walk the dog and put him to bed, then come to the bedroom naked and ready to forget his safe word."

Jeremy's skin warmed, excitement making his heart race and his dick harden. Just like that. Every damn time.

"Yes, Master Finn."

Owen grinned, pulling him closer for a kiss. "That's what I like to hear."

THANKS FOR READING!

I truly hope you enjoyed this book. If so, please leave a review and tell your friends. Word of mouth and online reviews are immensely helpful to authors and greatly appreciated.

To keep up with all the latest news about RG's books, release info, exclusive excerpts and more, check out her website RGAlexander.com. Stop by her group blog, Smutketeers.com to enter the frequent *contests* and *free book giveaways* each month.

Friend me on **Facebook**
https://www.facebook.com/RGAlexander.RachelGrace
to join **The Brass Chattery**
https://www.facebook.com/groups/292493407577385/
for contests, and smutty fun.

Kinda broad at the shoulder and narrow at the hip...

Trudy Adams never planned on going home again. Not to that sleepy little Texas town where everyone knew her business and thought she was trouble. She ran away to California years ago, and now, after what has felt like a lifetime of struggling, her lucky break might finally be around the corner.

And then she got that email.

John Brown has been waiting patiently for Trudy to return, but his patience has run out. He's had years to think about all the things he wants to do to her, and he's willing to use her concern for her brother, her desire to help her best friend get her story, and every kinky fantasy Trudy has to show her who she belongs to.

The explosive chemistry between them is unmistakable. But will history and geography be obstacles they can't overcome? When Trouble makes a two-week deal with Big Bad...anything can happen.

Warning: **READ THIS!** BDSM, explicit sex, voyeurism, accidental voyeurism, voyeurism OF voyeurism with a sprinkle of m/m, exhibitionism, ropes, cuffs, gratuitous spanking, skinny dipping, irresponsible use of pervertables...and a big, dirty man who will melt your heart.

Mr. Big Stuff
Bigger in Texas series, Book Two

Fifteen minutes was all he needed to get sick of the spotlight... One hot, hard ride was all it took to addict him to Sweet Caroline. How long will it take for her to give in?

New York Times and USA Today Bestselling Author

R.G. Alexander

Available Now!
www.RGAlexander.com

Mr. Big Stuff...who do you think you are?

Caroline Aaron has kissed a lot of frogs. The last

thing she needs is some cowboy-turned-reality star promising to come after her with his dangerous dimples and wicked smile. Especially not when the cowboy is eleven years younger, the brother of her best friend and doesn't meet any of the requirements on her List. Still, when he doesn't show up after she's waited three months to knock him down, it puts a dent in her pride.

And then Trudy asks for that favor…

For Jefferson Adams, fifteen minutes of fame was more than enough. All he wanted was Caroline but his dreams of the California girl got temporarily sidetracked. When she shows up in his life again, he's willing to do whatever it takes to make her his.

Warning: This won't be an average romance. Instead of flowers she'll get spankings. Instead of candlelight? A violet wand. Instead of fifteen minutes…she'll need forever.

Did I mention the rope? The wedding?

Glass slipper shopping can be a dangerous pastime…

The CEO's Fantasy-Book 1

Dean Warren is the billionaire CEO of Warren Industries. He's spent the last five years proving his worth and repairing his family's reputation. But the rules he's had to live by are starting to chafe, especially when it comes to one particular employee. He doesn't believe in coincidence, but when Sara Charles shows up suddenly unemployed and asking him to agree to a month of indulging their most forbidden fantasies--there's no way he can refuse.

When reality is better than his wildest dreams, will the CEO break all of his own rules to keep her?

The Cowboy's Kink-Book 2

Tracy Reyes is a man who enjoys having control. Over his family's billion dollar land and cattle empire, over the women he tops at the club, and over his life. When teacher Alicia Bell drops into his lap with a problem that needs solving and a body that begs to be bound, he can't resist the opportunity to give her the education in kink she needs. But can he walk away from his passionate pupil when it's time to meet his future bride?

The Playboy's Ménage-Book 3

Henry Vincent and Peter Faraday have been friends forever. The royal rocker and polymath playboy have more than a few things in common. They're both billionaires, they both love a challenge...and they've both carried a long-lasting torch for the woman that got away. Finding Holly again brings back feelings and memories neither one of them wanted to face. But they'll have to if they want to share her. Keeping her from running again and making her admit how she feels about them will take teamwork. Hours of teamwork...and handcuffs.

The Bachelors

We know every debutante's mama wants a piece of their action, but if you could choose without repercussions, which of the Billionaire Bachelors would be your fantasy? The true hardcore cowboy who has enough land and employees to start his own country, but no dancing partner for his special kind of two-step? The musician with a royal pedigree, a wild streak and a vast fortune at his disposal, who's never been seen with the same woman twice? His best jet-setting buddy who can claim no less than five estates, four degrees and three charges of lewd public behavior on his record? Or the sweet-talking, picture-perfect tycoon-cum-philanthropist who used to be the baddest of the bunch but put those days behind him when he took over as CEO of his family's company? (Or did he?)

Pick your fantasy lover--rocker, rancher, rebel or reformed rogue. Glass slipper shopping is a dangerous sport to be sure, especially with prey as slippery as these particular animals, but I'll still wish all my readers happy hunting.

From Ms. Anonymous

Available Now!

www.RGAlexander.com

OTHER BOOKS FROM R.G. ALEXANDER

Fireborne Series
Burn With Me
Make Me Burn
Burn Me Down-coming soon

Bigger in Texas Series
Big Bad John
Mr. Big Stuff-
Big Trouble-*coming soon*

The DD4 Series
Dirty Delilah

Billionaire Bachelors Series
The CEO's Fantasy
The Cowboy's Kink
The Playboy's Ménage

Children Of The Goddess Series
Regina In The Sun
Lux In Shadow
Twilight Guardian
Midnight Falls
Eternal Guardian

Wicked Series
Wicked Sexy
Wicked Bad
Wicked Release

Shifting Reality Series
My Shifter Showmance
My Demon Saint
My Vampire Idol

Temptation Unveiled Series
Lifting The Veil
Piercing The Veil
Behind The Veil

Superhero Series
Who Wants To Date A Superhero?
Who Needs Another Superhero?

Kinky Oz Series
Not In Kansas
Surrender Dorothy

More Than Ménage
Truly Scrumptious
Three For Me?
Four For Christmas
Marley in Chains

Anthologies
Three Sinful Wishes
Wasteland - Priestess
Who Loves A Superhero?
A Kinky Christmas Carol - Marley in Chains
Midnight Ink - Boxed Set

Bone Daddy Series
Possess Me
Tempt Me
To The Bone

Elemental Steam Series Written As Rachel Grace
Geared For Pleasure

ABOUT R.G. ALEXANDER

R.G. Alexander (aka Rachel Grace) is a *New York Times* and *USA Today* Bestselling author who has written over 30 erotic paranormal, contemporary, sci-fi/fantasy books for multiple e-publishers and Berkley Heat. Both her personalities are represented by the Brown Literary Agency.

She is a founding member of The Smutketeers, an author formed group blog dedicated to promoting fantastic writers, readers and a positive view of female sexuality.

She has lived all over the United States, studied archaeology and mythology, been a nurse, a vocalist, and now a writer who dreams of vampires, witches and airship battles. RG feels lucky every day that she gets to share her stories with her readers, and she loves talking to them on twitter and FB. She is happily married to a man known affectionately as The Cookie—her best friend, research assistant, and the love of her life. Together they battle to tame the wild Rouxgaroux that has taken over their home.

Sign up for the Smutketeers Newsletter
http://eepurl.com/OBKSD
for updates on contest giveaways and
New Releases.
All for Smut and Smut for All!

To Contact R. G. Alexander:
www.RGAlexander.com
www.RachelGraceRomance.com
www.Smutketeers.com
Facebook:
http://www.facebook.com/RachelGrace.RGAlexander
Twitter: https://twitter.com/RG_Alexander

Made in the USA
Middletown, DE
11 December 2015